STOP FAKING FOR STRIPES

THREE SHORT STORIES

ROMEO CONWAY

Order this book online at www.trafford.com
or email orders@trafford.com

Most Trafford titles are also available at major online book retailers.

Print information available on the last page.

ISBN: 978-1-6987-0385-5 (sc)
ISBN: 978-1-6987-0384-8 (hc)
ISBN: 978-1-6987-0386-2 (e)

Library of Congress Control Number: 2020921557

Trafford rev. 10/28/2020

 www.trafford.com

North America & international
toll-free: 844-688-6899 (USA & Canada)
fax: 812 355 4082

CONTENTS

STOP FAKING FOR STRIPES

SUNSET

THE BLOWER

STOP FAKING FOR STRIPES

FOR STRIPES

ROMEO CONWAY

CONCRETE

Bobby Lee stood out on the wicked and dangerous street corner of Denker and 101st Streets. This was the main hangout and street corner of the murderous Concrete Block Crip Gang. He watched cars zoom down the street while he waited nervously for his best and closest homeboy, Killa, to come out of that hood rat CeCe's house, which rested slightly off the corner of 101st Street. Bobby hated to wait, especially when there was work to be put down, not because he was doing the work, but more so because he did not want to be anywhere around the penal-risking activities in the first place.

Killa stepped out of CeCe's house and slammed the iron screen door shut. He zipped the front of his pants up, then he pulled a pack of Newport filtered cigarettes from his back pocket. He tapped the pack on his wrist, freeing a single cigarette, and returned the pack back to his pocket.

"What's up, cuzz?" Killa asked as he stepped from CeCe's front lawn to the sidewalk next to Bobby. Bobby frowned while his friend lit up the cigarette with a blue BIC lighter he fished out of his front pocket.

"What we waitin' on, cuzz?" Bobby asked.

Killa did not bother to respond. He took several long drags off the cancer stick then grabbed his crotch. "Damn, nigga, CeCe got the bomb, I don't know why you won't hit," Killa said, passing Bobby the cigarette. Bobby hated smoking. He never smoked the poison, but he took the cigarette from Killa and put it to his lips. Holding it between his middle and index fingers, he sucked the poison into his mouth, making sure he did not inhale.

A blue Ford sped down Denker, and Killa went for the .357 revolver in the waistband of his jeans just in case the car's occupants were rivals. While Killa's attention was on the car, Bobby blew the unrecycled smoke into his face. It was one of Bobby's best tricks to make Killa think he was smoking when he wasn't. That was Bobby at his best—instead of saying he didn't smoke, he would rather pretend he did. When the Ford sped off, providing no threat, Killa turned back to Bobby. "Why you always blowin' smoke in my face, nigga?" Killa said, stuffing the .357 back down his pants.

"You trippin', loc. What we waitin' on? It looks like it's about to rain," Bobby said, looking up to the sky as the clouds got darker and it got later in the evening.

"We waitin' on the homie Baby Bosco. Cuzz will be here," Killa said, walking over to his black turbo V6 1988 Grand National sitting sinisterly in CeCe's driveway on seventeen-inch gold Daytons. Bobby followed behind him and stood watch, looking up and down the street while Killa opened up the car's trunk, dug in, and pulled out a MAC-10.

"Where is this nigga, cuzz?" Bobby asked again. Killa closed the car trunk and sat down on top of the back bumper. He held up his palm to Bobby while gripping the MAC-10 in the other hand.

"Just calm down, cuzz, take yo mind off the bidness. That's why you should of waxed CeCe wit all that bumpa," he said, trying to smooth Bobby's nerves.

What? Bobby thought. He had known Killa since they were seven years old, and he had never known Killa for being calm or having patience.

A light rain started to fall on the two young men. "Damn, cuzz," Bobby complained. Killa smiled at his good friend.

"It's a good day for a murder," Killa said as a navy-blue 1982 Cadillac Coupe Deville cruised to a stop in front of CeCe's house. The car's driver got out of the Cadillac and walked over to the driveway where Bobby and Killa stood.

"Big K, cuzz, I got this gee-ride. What ya'll think, big homie?" Baby Bosco asked, smiling, filled with excitement.

"Yeah, that's cool, cuzz," Killa said, commending the up-and-coming hood star. After all, it was what the young boy strived for—acceptance and praise from the older homies, the original young gee he had one day hope to become. Bobby shook his head, wrapped in his own thoughts. When he was Baby Bosco's age, he was doing a stint in CYA for manslaughter, which made him hope Bosco would not take the same twisted and shifty road he took to live life. Still as much as Bobby hoped, Bosco did not follow in his footsteps. He hoped even more that he wouldn't be caught doing any work and end up in prison or on death row. Bobby's second plan far outweighed his hopes for Bosco, so when Killa handed Bobby a pair of gloves and the MAC-10, Bobby handed the gun to Bosco.

"Aye, Killa, cuzz, we already got our stripes. Let little cuzz get a chance to shine. It's his time," Bobby said, pointing at Bosco.

"Yeah, cuzz, you right, loc, but I'm go dump too. Niggas blasted the homie, cuzz, and I got to do something," Killa said, putting on a pair of brownies gardening gloves. "You drive, Bobo, and you get in the front seat, Baby Bosco. You ever shot a gun, little nigga? And don't lie," Killa asked the teen, who shook his head. Killa frowned as Bobby snickered at the youthful inexperience of Baby Bosco.

"Look, cuzz, you just stick that muthafucka out the window, aim, and shoot. It's gon' explode in yo hand, so use two to keep it steady. Kill as many of them niggas as you can, cuzz. They shot the homie, and, nigga, you can't claim Concrete if you ain't no killa! Is you with this?" he asked.

"Yeah, cuzz. I'm down, nigga," Bosco said.

Bobby sighed a big sigh of relief now that he was off the trigger. Bobby took one last look at Killa as he got into the driver's seat of the Cadillac and Killa slid into the back seat. *This man is the fuckin' devil,* Bobby thought. Bobby even thought Killa looked like the devil.

Killa was a small man in height, standing at five foot seven inches; he weighed in at a solid 140 pounds of solid muscle mass. He had long, black, curly hair that hung to his shoulders. His skin complexion was the color of bronze that displayed the tattoos that covered every inch of his arms and upper body. Killa had every one of his enemigo sets on his forearm with Xs striking them out, but what truly made Killa look like Lucifer himself to Bobby was the hazel eyes that shined like rubies when Killa got angry.

When Bosco got into the passenger seat and closed the car door, Bobby put the already running car into gear and sped off toward Normandie down 101st Street. He pushed the Cadillac through the rain-slickened, darkening streets, patrolling the turf of their most hated rivals, the Ninety-Seventh Street Suicidal Crip Gang. Bobby looked over at Baby Bosco, who seemed to be calm and enjoying the ride, with the MAC-10 in his hands. Bobby continued to drive, letting his thoughts get the best of him. Damn, here this fourteen-year-old kid about to do a drive-by, and he is just sitting here stone-faced. When I was his age, I was a nervous wreck, and I wasn't even doing the shooting on my first move." He wished he didn't have to be involved in this move in the first place, but he knew the Suicidals came through the night before and put four AK rounds through YG Bert Loc, and Killa would not let that ride. He also knew he could not let Killa down now that he was the driver of a potential murder mission. *Damn!* he thought.

"Bobo, buss a left on Ninety-Seventh!" Killa directed from the back seat. Bobby made a smooth left off Normandie onto Ninety-Seventh Street. Killa adjusted himself in the back seat. Bosco rolled down the electric window as they eyed two men walking from the corner liquor store in baggy clothing. One of the men wore a blue-and-gray Dallas Cowboy football jersey with a 97 on it, gray pants, blue Chuck Taylors, and a blue beanie. The man closest to the street had on a pair of gray dickies, a big, puffy Cowboys jacket, blue Jumpmans, and a blue Dallas hat. He put the forty-ounce of Old English still in the paper bag to his lips as Bobby turned off the Cadillac lights. The Cadillac crept like a vicious tiger stalking its prey. When Bobby pulled the car to a stop next to the two unsuspecting men, Killa stuck his body halfway out the car and aimed the .357 magnum at the man drinking the OE. Killa pulled the trigger, and a loud explosion followed. The bullet flew from the gun with blinding speed and tore into the skull of the forty-ounce drinker. Killa squeezed the trigger again, sending another round into the man's chest, his comrade tried to run for cover, but Baby Bosco stuck the MAC-10 out of the window with two hands and mowed him down with ten rounds. Both men were dead before they hit the sidewalk.

"Go, nigga! Go, cuzz!" Killa shouted at Bobby from the back seat. Bobby slammed his foot down hard on the gas pedal, sending the big car flying down toward Halldale.

"Hey, is that, that nigga Lil Mumu?" Killa pointed at a man out crossing Halldale going east on Ninety-Seventh with a woman.

"Yeah, that's cuzz and his baby mama," Bobby answered, heading toward the couple.

"Slow down, cuzz, and drive up closer to the curb," Killa instructed. Bobby did as he was told, and when they were side by side, Killa leaned back out the car window and squeezed the gun's trigger four times. The sounds of the thunderous pistol and the woman's screams disturbed the otherwise still of the rain-filled night, as Mumu died in her arms.

Bobby drove across Century into his neighborhood with a speed unseen in a car as big as the Cadillac did. When he pulled the car to a stop at the curb in front of CeCe's house, Bobby jumped out and tried to shake off what was left of the nerves and jitters he had. Killa and Bosco stepped out of the car with the guns in hand, hanging to their sides. Bobby noticed Killa had a wild grin on his face. He put his arm around the back of Bosco's neck, who also wore a sly smile on his face. Bobby looked deep into Bosco's eyes, but he did not find what he was looking for. There was no sign of remorse or recognition in regard for the murderous acts he had just participated in. No, Bosco was nothing like what Bobby thought he was. This kid was like Killa. This kid was the devil's offspring. Always the opportunist, Bobby's thoughts went to how he could use the murderous Bosco in the future. Maybe even against Killa, he thought, as he watched Killa pour more affection into the teen.

"You're a ridah, little cuzz. You should change yo name to Lil Killa. You got it in you, loc," he said.

"Hey, Killa, cuzz, I got to get back to the tilt. I got some shit I got to take care of," Bobby said, walking over to Killa's car in the driveway.

"Yeah, all right, Bobo, hold on real quick." Killa turned his attention back to Baby Bosco. "Aye, cuzz, take the car and dump it on the other side of Normandie. Give me that Mac, and, cuzz, don't tell nobody what we did tonight. I mean nobody, cuzz," he advised, taking the MAC-10 from the boy's hand. Bosco nodded his head as Killa spoke to him, then he threw up their neighborhood gang sign and walked over to the blue Cadillac. He slid behind the wheel of the big car, put it in gear, and sped off in the rain down 101st Street. Killa walked to CeCe's house and knocked on her iron screen door. Bobby opened the passenger side of Killa's car and got inside to wait for him.

"What's up, baby? I thought you were gone for the night," CeCe said, licking her lips as she opened the front door.

Killa stayed on the front porch, looking CeCe up and down. *Damn, she is thick as a horse,* he thought. "CeCe, hold these guns. I'll be back latah. I got to roll," he said, putting the two pistols into her hands." He spun on his heels and walked over to his car.

"Aye, wait, Killa, who you got with you? When you coming back?" she called after him.

Killa got into his car, ignoring her. He started the car up, pulled out the driveway, and slung the Grand National down Denker toward Century, getting sideways on the slick streets headed for Inglewood. As he navigated through the wet streets of South Central, Los Angeles, he lit up a Newport and took a long drag. He lowered the music from his brain-rattling max volume. As the beat went down, Killa looked over at Bobby, who was watching the land roll by out the passenger window.

"Aye, Bobby, that little nigga is a ridah, huh?" Killa asked as they came to a stop in front of the apartment. Bobby was staying with his overweight and oversexed Mexican girlfriend in Inglewood.

"Yeah, cuzz, I'll holla at you in a minute, loc," Bobby said as he got out of the car. He walked around to the driver's side of the car.

Killa lowered the window. "You know the homie Wack Wack is getting out the Y this weekend, and we're supposed to throw a welcome home party at CeCe's for cuzz," Killa said over the rumbling car engine. Both Killa and Bobby had been in YA with Wack Wack. Killa loved Wack Wack because they were two of the same people. They both were wild, crazy, and dangerous young gees without a heart. Bobby, on the other hand, hated Wack Wack, mostly because Wack Wack kept him in as much trouble in YA as Killa did on the street. There was that, and there was the fact that Wack Wack knew all his darkest secrets, unlike anybody else, that Bobby had faked his way through YA. "So you going or what, cuzz?" Killa asked, snapping Bobby back into reality.

"Naw, cuzz, I'm cool." The last place he wanted to be was around Wack Wack.

Killa frowned. "Man, cuzz Bobo, you need to let that YA shit go. We all homies just roll with me, I'm not go stand for any bullshit amongst homies Crip," he said, hoping he had gotten through to his best roll dog.

"All right, I'll be there. Ten first," Bobby said, flashing the 101st Street gang sign with his left hand. Killa flashed the sign, turned the music back up full blast, and drove off, leaving Bobby in the rain.

Bobby checked his pager for the time. It was 9:00 p.m. He wished it were later so that his live-in nympho would be asleep. He hated having sex with the woman, but he knew she was keeping him off the street and sex was all he had to offer. Bobby walked into the living room of the apartment, and all the lights were off. He took off his shirt, pants, and shoes, and he laid them on the couch armrest. Bobby thought if he stripped down first, he might be able to slide into bed without waking up Mary. He would have no such luck that night.

As he came into the bedroom, he saw Mary sitting on top of the bed naked with a towel underneath her legs, masturbating.

Damn. Bobby cringed inside. He had just interrupted her masturbation session, and he knew he was going to have to participate. He looked at Mary in disgust. There was nothing about her that was at all attractive to him. Her body was a mess, Mary had breast the size of volleyballs with long nipples that looked like erasers. She had a roll of flab around her stomach with a flat butt, which gave her an odd look. What even made her look worse were the small chicken legs she got around on. Mary's only upside was her long, black, curly hair that hung past her hips and matched her dark eyes. Her nose was slim and her lips were full, giving her a halfway decent face. Her best attributes was her large bank account and apartment. Still, it was not just Mary's appearance that disgusted Bobby. It was the fact that he had to have sex with her. He shed his boxers and crawled into the bed next to Mary. She took over instantly, pawing at him. *Damn, I hate this shit,* Bobby thought.

"I've missed you all day," she hissed into his ear. After the grueling foreplay session that seemed to go on for hours, Mary straddled him and hopped up and down on him until she reached climax. Before she could get excited again, Bobby faked an orgasm and pushed her off him.

"I'm tired, Mary, I need some rest," he said, rolling over and closing his eyes. Before Mary could respond, he had passed out from exhaustion.

Bobby tossed and turned in his sleep. He saw himself in his dream as a thirteen-year-old child behind the wheel of a stolen 1992 Ford Explorer. Bobby could barely see over the truck's hood.

"I can't see over the hood, cuzz!" Bobby shouted to Killa, who sat in the passenger seat of the SUV, holding a fully loaded TEC-9.

"Cuzz, just drive, I'm going to do the shootin'," Killa said.

"Cuzz, I just don't want to crash!" Bobby exclaimed, getting a tighter grip on the wheel.

"Look, Bobo, it's just point A to point B. This is the mission that's gon' put us on the map," Killa said, jacking a round into the TEC-9.

"All right, loc," Bobby said, pushing the truck across Normandie onto Ninety-Ninth Street and into the Cyco Gangsta Crip hood. When Bobby turned on to Budlong, he spotted an old friend, Tewy Loc, who was claiming the Cyco Gangsta Crip set. Killa spotted him also, recognizing Tewy Loc from their eighth-grade year at Bret Heart Junior High School.

"Aye, pull up on Tewy so I can blast, cuzz." Killa instructed. Bobby didn't think Killa should shoot Tewy Loc. After all, they were just friend less than a year ago, and now Killa wanted to kill him over a street war.

How can I do this without lookin' like a bitch? he asked himself. *I'm about to kill cuzz on Concrete Gaaaang!* Bobby found himself in a state of panic; he knew he had to act fast before Killa made his threat a promise. Bobby slammed his foot down on the pedal out of desperation, sending the Explorer shooting down Budlong.

"Cuzz, what the fuck?" Killa shouted as he was tossed back into his seat. Bobby raced northbound on Budlong blindly and ran smack into an older man crossing Ninety-Eighth Street. The body flew up into the air and came down into the truck windshield on the passenger side.

"Aaaah shit!" Bobby shrieked, slamming down on the truck's brakes.

When the truck stopped, Killa got out of the truck and pulled the dead man off the hood and windshield. Dropping the lifeless body to the street, he looked down at the corpse's face as Bobby tried to get his composure inside the truck.

"Cuzz, you just ran down Big Haunchie Bear. You killed a triple OG from GC," Killa said, getting back into the truck.

"I know I seen that nigga from Ninety-Ninth. That's why I shook Tewy cuzz," Bobby said, driving back to his hood.

In his dream, he saw the events unfold just as they transpired in real life. He saw himself getting his respect from all his homies since he told everybody that he killed Haunchie on purpose, and Killa backed his tale. Then he saw himself being arrested three weeks later after Tewy Loc told the authorities that Bobby had run over his big homeboy.

Bobby told his tale of events to the judge at the Inglewood Juvenile Court, and since Bobby never had a record, he was found guilty of involuntary manslaughter and given six years to be served in the California Youth Authority program. In his dreams, Bobby could hear the white judge's voice. "Bobby Lee, vehicular manslaughter, six years in the CYA—six years in California State Prison. Bobby, you are sentenced to life in the California State Prison system," the judge chanted.

"Aaah!" Bobby screamed, shooting up in the bed, waking up Mary. He looked around the dark room lit only by the television.

"Bobby, baby, what's wrong, Daddy?" Mary asked.

Bobby shook his head. "Nothin'. I'm cool, cuzz," he said, lying back down.

"Good then," Mary said, stroking him between his legs; Bobby was not in the mood. Mary readjusted in the bed to give him some dome action. Bobby could not fake his arousal, but he had to focus, or he would lose himself looking at the flab flapping around her body. Mary went to work like a real pro until Bobby spewed his load.

She wiped her mouth and smiled. "I'm glad you like that Bobby, because now it's Mama's turn," she said, straddling his face.

Fuck! Fuuuck! his mind screamed. He hated when she made him go down on her. He felt like vomiting when he tasted her juices in his mouth. *Fuck this, I got to get out of here. I got to get out of her debt. I got to get some cheese. Fuck Mary. Tomorrow, I'm out of here,* he thought.

KILLA'S ADVOCATE

Bobby woke up with an attitude from the night before. He put his hand to his mouth and blew his breath into his palm. His face twisted into a frown as he inhaled the stench of Mary's nectar and morning breath. He climbed out of the bed and dragged himself to the bathroom to brush his teeth and take a shower. When Bobby got out of the shower, he put on a T-shirt and boxers. He had to stay covered up because he could not afford Mary being aroused at the sight of his body.

He strode into the dining room and sat down at the dinner table. He picked up the day's *Los Angeles Times* and turned to Sports section. Mary finished cooking his favorite breakfast, as she did every morning before she went to work. The smell of steak, eggs, hash browns, and coffee filled his nostrils as Mary sat the plate and mug down in front of him. Bobby kept reading the paper as he dug into his meal with his offhand. Then he folded the paper in half and sat it on the table. Mary leaned over and gave him a kiss on the cheek.

"I'm heading off to work, baby, I'll see you later," she said, heading for the front door.

"Hold up, I need some money and the jeep keys," Bobby said around a mouth full of eggs and steak. Mary stopped in her tracks. She dug into her purse and pulled out a roll of hundreds, fifties, and twenties. She peeled off three hundreds and handed them to him, and then she pulled the keys to the Jeep Wrangler out of her purse and sat them on the end of the table. "Good lookin' out," Bobby called after her as she walked out of the door.

After he ate his breakfast, Bobby went back into the bedroom to get dressed. He put on a blue, black, and gray Ralph Lauren long-sleeved flannel shirt, blue 501 Levis, and blue-and-white Air Jordans. Mary had bought all his clothes and shoes. *Too bad she is such a slut,* he thought.

Bobby thought back to how he ended up with Mary in the first place. Mary was Killa's girlfriend when they were in Inglewood High School, before Mary got all fat and let her body go. When Killa went to YA, Mary wrote and visited him for his whole four years, and when Killa paroled, he came home to Mary. Mary spent money left and right on Killa. She bought him clothes, shows, jewelry, and then a Grand National. After Killa got back on his feet, he moved out of Mary's house with her mom and got back with his wife. Mary had just moved into her own apartment when Bobby wrote Killa saying he didn't have a place to stay when he got out of YA. Killa told him he had a place for him to rest with a cool girl who would look out for him. So when Bobby paroled, he moved into her apartment.

Bobby looked himself over in the bedroom dresser mirror. His hair was wavy, cut low evenly. His eyebrows were thick, and he wore a thick mustache and a thin beard. He had big lips a wide nose and a dark-brown complexion. Bobby put two earring studs in his ears, the diamond studs winking back at Bobby in the mirror. He put on his blue Los Angeles Dodgers hat and gold Rolex chain Mary had bought him. Even in his clothes, you could see the juvenile system had done a lot for his physical appearance.

When Bobby went to YA, he was a slim 107 pounds at five feet six inches tall with twelve-inch thick arms. Now he was 195 pounds and stood five feet ten inches with seventeen-inch thick arms. Bobby had become a monster in stature, but his heart had never changed. Bobby put the three hundred dollars into his pocket and walked out of the apartment.

Bobby walked into the apartment complex's underground parking structure. Mary's gray 1995 Jeep Wrangler was in the parking stall. Mary had taken her 1997 Lexus to work. Bobby checked around the structure for danger. There was none. He opened up the car door and got inside. He put the key in the ignition and started up the jeep. He put C-Bo's *Tales from the Crypt* CD into the CD player, closed the jeep door, backed out of the parking stall, and headed to his hood.

When Bobby got to his homeboy G Ball's house, he saw Killa's Grand National glistening out on the curb in front of G Ball's yard. Bobby pulled into the driveway behind Lil Rah Rah's orange-candy-painted two-door 1986 Chevy Caprice. All his homies always hung out at G Balls house. Big Gang Ball was only a few years older than Bobby was, but he was one of the first original young gees of their set so all the YGs, even Killa, respected G Ball as a OYG homie.

Bobby got out of the jeep and strode across the front lawn to G Ball's front door. He tried the knob and turned it. Once he realized it was unlocked, he walked through the house G Ball's mother had left him when she died, but there was no one inside. He went into the kitchen and pulled a beer out of the refrigerator, then he walked out to the backyard.

"What's up, cuzz?" Lil Rah said, greeting Bobby as he walked into the backyard. He sat on an old soft, black chair while Killa and G Ball stretched out on two flimsy aluminum lawn chairs on the grass, drinking beers. Bobby walked over and took a seat on an old rundown recliner chair next to Rah Rah.

"Shit, it ain't nothing. You know a nigga tryna chase some paper," he said, taking a swig of the beer.

Killa had a confused look on his face. "Paper fa'what, cuzz? Mary ain't actin', right, cuzz? I'll come over there and—"

"Naw, cuzz, you trippin'. I need my own shit," Bobby said, cutting Killa off before he got all excited. Killa, Rah Rah, and G Ball broke out into a fit of laughter. "What's funny, cuzz?" Bobby asked not amused.

"Mary makin' you get a nine-to-five." Rah Rah giggled.

Naw, nigga. I'm tired of that bitch raping and abusing me, Bobby thought, but instead he said, "Naw, I just wanna get deeper in the game, get a whip and a spot."

"Why you won't tell Big Cisco to front you a half a brick?" G Ball suggested.

"And then what?" Bobby asked.

"Chunk it, nigga. That shit movin' like hotcakes at Taco's spot," Rah Rah informed him.

"Wicked and Man Man came through here from Park Block, lookin' for some work. You know Wicked? Cuzz got that white '88 Monte Carlo," G Ball said. Bobby nodded. "But how you gon' get the seven three to pay the homeboy back?" he asked Bobby.

"Cuzz, fuck Cisco, you ain't got to pay that nigga. That nigga's a bitch, cuzz, been scary ever since the Suicidals almost shot cuzz's leg off, and who had to ride for that fool? Me! That nigga owe the homies. Call cuzz, G Ball, and tell him to bring that half," Killa said.

"Why you tryin' to strip the homie, cuzz? You already pistol-whipped cuzz and took his AK," G Ball asked.

Bobby didn't like when Killa got excited because it usually involved him. Killa picked up a brown paper bag from the side of his lawn chair. Inside of the bag were the remains of the forty ounce he had been drinking. He put the bottle to his lips and tossed his neck back, swallowing the last of the amber liquid. Bobby was hoping things didn't blow up between the two of his homies.

"What up, cuzz? Bobo, Big G Ball, Killa, Rah Rah!" Baby Bosco shouted as he and Lil Criptanite came walking down the driveway into the backyard.

"Cuzz, don't say nothin' to that nigga, Ball. Cuzz ain't the homie," Killa said, slamming down the paper bag, busting the glass all over the grass. The two TGs looked from Killa to G Ball and G Ball to Killa.

"Cuzz, what?" G Ball asked, getting up from his lawn chair.

"Nigga, you heard me, you busta ass nigga. When the last time you put in some work for Concrete Gang? Nigga, you haven't," Killa said, pulling a big 9 mm out of the waistband of his creased, blue khaki shorts.

Damn, Bobby thought, jumping up from the beat-up recliner and standing between Killa and G Ball. *God, please don't let this happen,* he prayed inside. "Killa, cuzz, you trippin'. This is the OYG homie," Bobby said.

"Fuck all that. Cuzz gonna help us strip out Cisco, or I'm stainin' cuzz back here like a nigga stained them 'Sewercidals.' This nigga ain't no true young gee," Killa said, buzzing off the forty.

Rah Rah stood up to help. "Wait a minute, Killa. Cuzz ain't say he wasn't gonna call. He just asked why you was strippin' out the homie," he appealed.

Killa spun the barrel of death around on Rah Rah. "Nigga, who asked you, bitch ass nigga?" Killa screamed.

Bobby stepped in again. "Hold up. G Ball, you gonna call or what?" Bobby asked in his last attempt to keep Killa from shooting up the whole backyard.

G Ball looked at Bobby then Killa and Rah Rah. "Yeah, I'll call, cuzz," he said, feeling somewhat defeated.

"See, it's all good, Killa, just kick back," Rah Rah said as Killa tucked the gun back into his pants. When G Ball walked back into the house to make the call, Killa grabbed Bobby in a headlock, tryin' to wrestle with his good friend. Bobby got free and shook off some of his nerves.

"If this nigga resist, I'm smoking cuzz right here on the set," Killa threatened. "What's up my little young nigga, Baby Bosco," he said, hugging the teen.

"We came over cuzz the homie Lil Crip wanted to put some work in," Baby Bosco said.

"Cuzz, ya'll know how to do it. Go put some work in block off some streets, yellow tape a nigga," Killa encouraged. Killa's word to the young boys went in one ear and out the other. Bobby was more worried about Killa robbing Big Cisco. The last time the two crossed paths, Bobby was in YA, but he heard Cisco had brought a new AK-47 to Lil Capone's house and told him to hold it while he left town. Killa borrowed the gun from his loyal YG comrade and shot down three Cyco Gangsta Crips at Red's Market on Century and Budlong. When Cisco returned for the gun, Killa told him he was keeping the K for the hood. Arguments followed. Killa pulled a .45 out of his pants and slapped Cisco across his old rubbery face with the pistol, busting open his skin. Killa didn't stop beating Cisco until Big Haymaker and Lil Trouble pulled him off him. Before he let that happen, Bobby would do the jack himself, he thought.

An hour later, Cisco pulled in front of G Ball's house in his white 1996 SS Chevy Impala on twenty-two-inch chrome blade rims. Bobby had a plan to keep Cisco away from Killa and get the dope on his own, so he told Killa he would be on the front porch talking with Baby Bosco. Bobby's plan may have worked if Cisco didn't blow the horn when he arrived, alerting Killa, Rah Rah, and Lil Criptanite also of his arrival. "Damn," Bobby said, his panic starting to get the best of him.

"You got a strap on you, little nigga?" he asked. *Please don't let me have to shoot this man,* he prayed to himself as Bosco handed him the small chrome .380 he pulled out the pocket of his blue hooded sweatshirt.

Killa, Criptanite, and Rah Rah had reached the porch where Bobby and Bosco awaited Cisco to get out the car.

"Killa, cuzz, I got this, don't even trip," Bobby said as Cisco got out of the Impala holding a black plastic bag in his hand. He made his way from the street to the grass.

"If cuzz acts up, smoke cuzz, or I will," Killa said as Bobby grabbed Bosco around the shoulder.

"Come on, Baby Bosco, I'm a show you how to do this shit," he said on the outside, but on the inside, where his heart was beating one hundred thousand beats per minute, he was saying, *Don't act up. Please don't act crazy, Cisco.*

Cisco smiled as he met Bobby and Baby Bosco in the middle of the yard. "What it do, Bobo cuzz? I ain't seen you in forever. What you do like eight years, you got big as fuck, little homie. I heard you been out there chippin' Sewercidals last night cuzz you got to kick back. I got that work for you to get back on your feet and get back at me," he said, handing Bobby the trash bag with the half a kilogram inside. "What's up, little homie?" Cisco said to Bosco.

"I ain't yo little homie, nigga," Bosco said, taking a step back from Cisco.

"What little nigga, I'm a gee," Cisco said, looking at Bosco, Bobby, and the men on the front porch. He put his hand to his forehead, feeling the scars Killa had left him with.

Damn, I don't want to do this shit. Fuck it, I got this, yeah, I got it on Concrete Gang. Hearing the words in his own mind even made Bobbie laugh. *Who am I kidding?* he thought. He turned around to take one last look at Killa, whose face was constricted in a frown, which meant Bobby had to do what he said he would do. He pulled the .380 from his pants and stuck the gun in Cisco's face. "Cuzz, give me all the money you got on you, cuzz," he demanded.

"Bobo, cuzz, what is this shit? Why you strippin' me out?" Cisco asked, holding his hands up in the air.

"Nigga, I ain't tryna hear that shit. Nigga, strip, give me everything, cuzz!" Bobby shouted, snatching the big gold Figaro link chain off Cisco's neck, shaking his head in disgust. Cisco went into his pockets and removed his money, phone, pager, and an ounce of chronic weed. Cisco kept his eyes on the barrel of the gun in Bobby's right hand as he handed Baby Bosco his belongings.

"Nigga, break off that Rolex too and the diamond earrings," Bobby said.

"Man, cuzz, we supposed to be homeboys," Cisco said, looking over Bobby's shoulder toward the porch at Killa, who now had a smile on his face. Cisco took off the watch and the earrings. *Yeah, that's right. Be cool, give us all that material shit. Don't make this fool Killa kill you,* Bobby thought.

"Strip that nigga all the way out, cuzz!" Killa shouted from the porch.

Damn, cuzz, Bobby thought. "Take all that shit off, nigga, to the socks," Bobby said.

Cisco started to take off his clothes. "Damn, cuzz, come on, Bobo, my gators, my fresh silk linen suit?"

Naw, cuzz, if it were up to me, you keep all yo shit, Bobby thought. "Nigga, shut the fuck up and take that shit off!" he ordered.

Cisco did as he was told until he stood in his socks and boxers only. Bobby and Bosco walked over to the Jeep Wrangler. Killa and Lil Criptanite walked by Cisco in the middle of the lawn, laughin' on the way to Killa's Grand National. Bosco put all the stolen property into the jeep.

"Baby Bosco, take cuzz's car. Nigga, you bet not report it stolen, Cisco," Killa said.

Bosco took the keys, went, and got into Cisco's impala. Bobby got into the jeep, and Killa and Criptanite got into the Grand National.

Killa pulled his car next to Bobby. "Roll over to Mary's cuzz," he said as though he were calling the shots. Bobby frowned, driving off.

Feeling the worst was over. Cisco flew into a rage and exploded on G Ball and Lil Rah Rah. "Cuzz, I'm a kill that nigga, Bobo! All them niggas is dead, loc! You niggas too, you bitch ass niggas set me up. Fuck ya'll!" Cisco shouted.

"Cuzz, what?" Lil Rah Rah said, coming off the porch. He crossed the grass in three long strides. When he stood before Cisco, he swung a hard right-handed hook that landed on Cisco's chin, knocking him out cold. Rah Rah got into his Chevy Caprice and drove away from G Ball's house, leaving Cisco asleep in the grass.

When Bobby and Killa walked into Mary's apartment, she was busy in the kitchen cooking dinner. She shot out of the kitchen when she saw Killa and Bobby step into the living room. She gave both men a hug and kissed Bobby on the lips. Mary walked back into the kitchen while Killa and Bobby plopped down on the couch. Killa put his feet up on the coffee table. Bosco and Criptanite knocked on the apartment door when they finished parking the Impala. Bobby got up from the couch and opened the door, letting the boys in. He went back and sat down on the couch next to Killa. The sight of Mary cooking in the kitchen greeted both Bosco and Criptanite. They studied her from afar, noticing how her large, heavy breast strained against the material of her short sundress, which exposed her skinny legs. Mary turned around from the stove, seeing the boys from their stalker's perch at the front door. She smiled and flipped her long, wavy hair over her left shoulder.

"Killa, are you all staying for dinner? Should I make them something too?" Mary asked.

"Yeah, cuzz, hook that shit up. You know how I like shit," Killa shouted from the couch.

Damn, why she ain't ask me? I'm the one who lives here! I got to fuck her stankin' ass twenty foe seven. Shit, it don't matter. I'll have my own shit soon, Bobby thought.

Bosco and Criptanite sat on a couch across from Bobby and Killa. Bosco knew Pam was Killa's main girl, and he knew Killa's wife. What he didn't know was who the chick in the kitchen with the huge rack was, but he sure wanted to know. "Aye, Kill, is that one of yo chicks?" he asked.

Killa shook his head. "Naw, cuzz, why? Ya'll like that?" Killa asked with a snicker and glanced over at Bobby. "That's Bobo's girl," he added.

"Cuzz, no it ain't. Fuck that bitch," Bobby said with a frown.

"Can we hit then?" Criptanite asked Bobby.

"I don't give a fuck. That bitch do what she wanna do," Bobby said.

When Mary was done setting the table, they went and took their seats. Bobby sat at the head of the table and started to eat the tacos

Mary made for them. Mary rubbed his shoulders and kissed his neck while looking at Killa across the table.

"Mary, come here," Killa demanded. Mary dropped Bobby like a bad habit and zoomed to Killa's side. Killa grabbed her by the back of her neck, pulling her face to his face. He started to whisper to her, "I want you to hook up my little homies."

"But, Killa, what about Bobby?" she asked, looking across the table.

"Cuzz ain't trippin'. I want you to do this for me," Killa said.

Mary nodded her head and headed for the bedroom. Even though she felt bad, she never let Killa down. "I'll see you later," she said to Bobby, who continued eating. "Bobby," she called louder at him.

"Yeah, do what you do. Later, cuzz," he said annoyed. *Bitch always callin' me Bobby in front of my homeboys,* he thought. Mary put her head down and closed the bedroom door behind her.

"Cuzz, ya'll hurry up and eat. She waiting on ya'll," Killa told the boys.

"Shit, I'm done now cuzz!" Criptanite said, getting up from the table.

"Me too, cuzz, let's go!" Bosco said. The two boys took off after Mary, crashing into each other on the way into the bedroom.

Bobby sat at the table, steaming within his own thoughts. Mary had confessed to him in the past that she still loved Killa, and no one had ever treated or made her feel how he did, but this, Bobby thought, was ridiculous. He could not believe Killa still had control over Mary as he did.

Damn, cuzz, Mary ain't all that bad. Maybe all I got to do is start actin' like Killa, and maybe she'll fall in line under me. Yeah, that's what I'll do, starting tomorrow. There's gonna be some changes for us round here, he thought.

"Aye, cuzz, that nympho bitch gonna work them young muthafuckas out, huh?" Killa said, laughing.

This nigga in my house callin' shots on my bitch, Bobby thought, fuming. "Yeah, cuzz, she's gonna flip them niggas," Bobby said. "Fuck that though, cuzz, we gotta chop down this brick."

3

MARY'S CHECK

Bobby sat on the living room couch counting the money he had taken out of Cisco's pockets and split it with Killa. He was not happy. Out of $3,000, he ended up with only $1,500 and a quarter kilo of rock. Killa had the other fourth.

All that work for this bullshit? This was a fuckin' one-man lick, Bobby thought, standing up from the couch so that he could stretch. His back was killing him from sleeping on the small sofa the night before. *Sure not sleeping on no skeet-stained bed with Mary's punk ass,* he thought as he twisted his upper body from right to left. At the mention of her name in his mind, Bobby frowned. Last night's memories flooded his mind. After Killa and Bobby broke down the rock, he had to listen to Mary's moans, screams, and whimpers of pleasure coming through the thin apartment walls. It was then that Bobby realized he didn't want Mary being flipped. He didn't want the boys having their way with her, fucking her like a motel slut, but Bobby knew it was too late to stop what he had already let set in motion by Killa, because for him, to do that meant he had to admit he cared about Mary, and he wasn't going to do that.

Bobby walked into the bedroom he shared with Mary. The bed was already made up with a fresh blanket and new sheets. Bobby heard the shower water running, then he checked the bedside clock on the nightstand. It read 6:15 a.m. on a Friday. Mary was supposed to be out of there by 5:00 a.m., and she didn't even have his breakfast ready. Bobby felt a light rage swelling inside of him.

I'm going to try this Killa shit on this bitch, and I hope it works because she can't keep on fuckin' dudes and livin' like this, he thought as he heard the shower water shut off. Mary stepped into the bedroom wearing a pink bath towel she could barely close because of her massive breast. "Hope this works," he mumbled as he walked around the bed and grabbed her by the arm before she could reach the closet.

"Where's my breakfast? You late for work and you ain't even cook for me!" he said.

Mary looked at him in an irritated manner. "I can't, Bobby, I'm running too late. You will have to get something at McDonald's," she said while yanking her arm out of his grasp. She looked at him standoffish.

What do I do? What would Killa do? he asked himself. "Bitch, if you weren't up all night hoing, you could have had yo ass up ready for work and my breakfast ready!" Bobby screamed.

Mary's face twisted into a frown. "Bobby, you need to calm down. I got to go to work," she said sternly.

Killa's method had better be right, Bobby thought as he reached back and slapped Mary across the face. "Bitch, that's another thang. Don't be callin' me Bobby around my homeboys," he shouted on the outside, while he said on the inside, he thought, *I'm sorry, Mary,* feeling bad for striking her.

Mary held her face where Bobby had struck her; her skin seemed to burn, but she found herself turned on by the newfound passion inside of Bobby. This wasn't the Bobby she was used to. He usually let her clothes free and have her way with him. *Today he's intense,* she thought. She didn't know what got into him, but she liked it.

"I'm sorry, Bobby, what do you want me to do?" Mary asked.

Damn, this shit is workin', Bobby thought. *I think I can work this a little while longer.* "You tell me what you want to do since you wanna act like a ho. You wanna be a ho? I will have you on Century flippin' tricks. You wanna turn tricks, Mary?" Bobby asked.

"Bobby, no! I-I-I just thought—"

"You thought what? That while I'm kickin' it with Killa, I want you fuckin' and suckin' my little homies, that's what you thought?" he asked, cutting her off. I said 'You do what you want to do'—that's what you wanted to do?"

Mary looked confused and flustered. "I know Bobby, I don't, I-I'm sorry," she said.

Damn, where did these feelings come from? Mary was just a place to stay, but now she was more like my girl. I like Mary in this submissive role, he thought. "It's gonna be some changes around here! Now cook my shit!" he screamed, flinching as though he would strike her again.

Mary cowered away all the while, wishing Bobby would hit her again. "All right, Bobby, let me get dressed first," she said, standing up from the bed, keeping the towel partially closed around her water-soaked body.

"Cook my shit in that now!" he said and walked into the bathroom to take a shower.

Mary watched Bobby as he strode off into the bathroom. It took all the self-control she could muster to keep her from jumping Bobby on the spot. Mary smiled to herself as she went to the kitchen to cook his breakfast.

Bobby got out of the shower and put on a pair of boxers and his blue house shoes. When he passed the sink, he got a glimpse of his tatted upper body in the mirror. He stopped to get a full look at himself. He saw the big CBC in Old English letters that covered his chest first. His name, Bobo, was stretched across his stomach. He turned to view the big blocked numbers 101, which stretched from his shoulders down his lower back, then he looked down at the two crossed-out three-letter abbreviation for the Suicidal Crip Gang and the Cyco Gangsta Crips on his forearm. Killa had pressured both him and Wack Wack in YA to get all Bs and all their enemies crossed out on their left forearms like his own. When Killa left Paso Robles, Bobby took several beatings from both the Suicidals and the Cyco Gangstas. Bobby even declined a few rumbles with this rivals, tired of getting his ass whipped. "Damn these tattoos," he said.

When Bobby took his seat at the head of the table, Mary was just finishing the last of his breakfast. His ritual morning paper was not at the table because Mary was running late. He looked at Mary over the stove with the towel barely clinging to her body with lust in his eyes; he got up from his chair and walked behind her as she started to load his fried steak onto his plate. Bobby felt himself starting to become excited. He grabbed Mary around the waist and pushed her against the hot stove.

"Bobby wait, what?" Mary asked, startled by Bobby's swift and forceful movements. He yanked the towel off her and plunged himself into her throbbing core. Bobby started to work himself into a frenzy as he moved in and out of her. Mary found herself in a state of bliss while Bobby went to work. He started to notice how excited Mary was getting by her screams of pleasure.

No! No! No! This shit is for me, me, me! he shouted inside, disengaging himself from Mary's center.

"Bobby, what? Why'd you stop?" Mary asked, looking over her shoulder. Bobby didn't bother to respond; instead, he repositioned himself using Mary's juices and squeezed back into her tightest region. "Ouch, Bobby, hold up!" Mary screamed.

"You'll get use to it," he said, and continued his movements inside of her. When Mary started to get back into the mood, Bobby came and went to his meal. Mary was sad since she had to go to work unsatisfied. She begged Bobby on her hands and knees for him to finish what he had started, but he refused. "I'm finished!" he said.

"Please, Bobby," Mary begged.

"You had enough last night, Mary," he said, making her feel real small. "Now it's check day, so you can't miss work. When you buss the check, I need you to bring me some money on 101st Street and Denker—you can't miss it."

Mary was in tears when she left the apartment for work. Bobby started to feel bad for her and for himself as he reflected. As Bobby started to reflect, fear started to arise within his mind. *I hope Mary ain't no psycho bitch that's going to get a knife and stab me while I'm sleep. Maybe I went too far,* he thought. He put on his clothes and went to his hood to hang out with Killa.

Bobby pulled the Jeep Wrangler to a stop in front of his homeboy Big Time Bomb's house on 101st Street and Budlong. Killa, Lil Criptanite, and Baby Bosco sat on the porch steps, smoking chronic blunts from the weed sack they took from Cisco a day earlier. Bobby parked Mary's jeep in the driveway behind Time Bomb's gold 1963 Chevy SS Impala low rider on gold Daytons. Bobby got out of the jeep and walked over to sit next to Lil Criptanite, who passed him the blunt. Bobby did his usual smoke trick.

"Damn, cuzz," Criptanite said as the smoke hit him in the face.

"Cuzz always do that shit," Killa said, starting to laugh.

'Cause I don't smoke, nigga, Bobby thought. "Just some shit I picked up, you know how niggas just be doing shit," he said, making the whole group erupt in laughter.

"Aye, cuzz, before you rolled up, the homies was telling me how they had Mary on smash, huh? Tell 'em, Lil Crip Crip!" Killa encouraged.

The last thing Bobby wanted to hear was this fifteen-year-old punk telling him how they had pounced, pawed, plunged, and spewed in his girlfriend, but he kept a smile of interest on his face to maintain his appearance of a heartless playboy.

"Yeah, Bobo, we had her on all foes. She was givin' a nigga some dome, and Bosco was hittin' it from the back, and I popped on them big-ass titties, cuzz," Criptanite was saying, but Bobby couldn't hear him anymore. *He drifted into his own thoughts. How this little nigga gonna just get at my girl like a ho, I wish I could have Killa kill this little nigga,* he thought as he studied Lil Criptanite while he spoke. The little skinny hood wore the gold chain Bobby had taken off Cisco's neck. The weed and the jewelry were all they had given to the two boys after the robbery. Bobby had also promised to give them the '96 impala, which was still parked at Mary's house, once he took off the rims and took out the sound system. Criptanite was not big in stature, but Bobby was sure he had a huge heart. He knew he had a big mouth after hearing him talk about Mary. He looked over Bosco, whom he knew had heart and was bigger than Criptanite was. Then it hit him. *I'm a muthafuckin' young gee, and what I say goes,* he thought.

"Aye, Killa, which one of these little niggas you think got more heart?" Bobby asked, cutting Criptanite's sexcapade in half.

Killa, always a man of drama, smiled. "Ain't nothing personal, Baby Bosco, I think Lil Crip can fade you," he said, laughin'.

"I got my money on Baby Bosco," Bobby said.

"What? Cuzz can't see me?" Criptanite said.

"Well, ya'll get down in the grass," Bobby said, hoping Criptanite got creamed.

The two youths got up from the porch and went onto Time Bomb's front lawn. They took their stances, balling up their fist. They circled each other closer and closer until Criptanite struck first, hitting Bosco in the eye. Bosco took the punch in stride and threw a punch or two back. Criptanite unloaded with a flurry of punches that had no effect. Bosco came back with his own flurry and knocked Criptanite to the lawn.

"Let cuzz get up," Killa said.

Bosco backed up and let him get back to his feet, and the two boys went at it again until Killa separated them and then made them shake hands.

"Aye, K, I'm 'bout to roll to the Park Blocks real quick to see if I can get this SS from Wicked. I'll catch you at CeCe's later tonight, cuzz. Baby Bosco, roll wit' me, cuzz," Bobby said, getting into the jeep. Bosco got into the passenger seat. *That's what that little loud mouth gets,* Bobby thought, looking at Criptanite's busted lip as he backed out of the driveway and took off toward Normandie.

Bobby and Bosco pulled to a stop at the curb in front of Wicked's house on 109th Street off Denker. Both Man Man and Wicked were shooting dice with a few of their homies in the driveway.

"Damn, cuzz, niggas just hit me for a gee," Wicked said as he rose from his crouched position to greet Bobby and Baby Bosco. "What's crackin', Bobo? What that Block like?" he said.

Bobby and Wicked had been good friends for years; they were bunkmates in Preston, and the Ten Nine Park Block Crips and the Ten First Concrete Block Crips were under the Block alliance. "What that Block like, cuzz," Bobby said, shaking Wicked's hand.

"You know it. What's up? Ya'll come to shoot dice or just kick it?" he asked.

"Naw, you still selling that MC?" Bobby asked.

"Yeah, cuzz, it's in the backyard. Come on, cuzz," Wicked said, leading the way by his homies and stopping at his backyard gate. When they got into the backyard, Wicked's tiger, a black-and-white striped pit bull, barked and growled next to the SS. The dog barked and strained against his chain as Bobby stepped up to view the car's interior. *Man, I hope that damn monster don't get off that damn chain,* he thought, scared to death.

"He tight, huh, cuzz?" Wicked asked.

Hell naw! Fuck naw! Cuzz, I would never have no fuckin' vicious killer like that for a fuckin' pet. No fuckin' way, Bobby's mind ranted. "Uh, oh yeah, cuzz, he straight," Bobby said, turning his attention back to the SS. *I need to get this and get the fuck out of there before this psycho mutt breaks his chain and have me for brunch.* The Monte Carlo SS had a glossy white pearl paint job, gray interior, and seventeen-inch gold Daytons on low-profile tires.

"I stripped out the beat, cuzz, but everything else is as a nigga see it. I'm just tryin' to put some rims on my Benz and some chips in my pocket, loc. What you want to do?" Wicked asked.

"I'll shoot you four zones, $1,500 and some twenty-two-inch blades," Bobby offered.

Wicked grabbed his chin and started stroking his goatee as he considered Bobby's proposal.

"Woof! Woof!" the dog barked. *Hurry up, nigga!* Bobby thought.

"All right, cuzz, we'll do the paperwork later," Wicked said, fishing the keys out of his pocket.

"I got the foe zones in the jeep, and I'll get you the rims tomorrow," Bobby said, going into his pocket and pulling out the $1,500 and handed it to Wicked as Wicked handed him the Monte Carlo keys.

Bobby rolled down Denker to 101st Street and parked in front of CeCe's house. Bosco followed behind him in Mary's jeep. When they got there, there were several of their older homeboys there and some of the YGs and TGs having a hood meeting. Bobby didn't want to be a part of the meeting they were having, mostly because he knew it would be drama. He wished Killa was there, but he didn't see his car. The meeting started good for Bobby. He was receiving praise for the murders Killa and Baby Bosco had done on the Suicidals, then the conversation shifted gears to Big Cisco. A heated argument broke out between Bobby, Big Lunatic, and Big G Loc, true Cisco supporters. Bobby seemed to be outweighed and outgunned—until Killa and Lil Criptanite rolled up in Big Time Bomb's six tray and joined in on the meeting and pulled out a strap on the OGs and rolled them up out of the meeting at CeCe's house.

After the meeting broke up, Killa and Bobby sat out on the front porch, drinkin' a forty ounce. Criptanite and Bosco were inside entertaining CeCe.

"Aye, cuzz, is that Mary?" Killa asked as he saw the blue Lexus pulling to a stop in front of Time Bomb's low rider.

"Yeah, that's her, cuzz," Bobby said, getting up from his seat and walking over to the car. Mary rolled down the window.

"Hi, baby," she said, handing Bobby $800 in cash. "That's half of $1,700. Are you coming home tonight? 'Cause I can cook," Mary asked.

"Yeah, I'll be there. Make chicken," Bobby said with a smile and leaned into the car to give her a kiss on the lips. When Mary drove off, Bobby went back and sat next to Killa.

"Damn, cuzz, you got that bitch in check. She gave you her money?" Killa asked

Nigga, get out my business, Bobby thought. "Yeah, you know I need half," he said.

"At least you let her keep half," Killa said.

Bobby smiled, pleased with himself.

WACK

Bobby woke up the next morning before the sun rose. Mary was still in the bed asleep next to him. He looked over at her as he slid out of the bed and put on his house shoes. He felt bad about the way he had been treating her, so he decide to try something new. He took a quick shower, then he got dressed in a pair of Old Navy blue jeans and a white Hanes T-shirt. He strolled into the living room and dug the four ounces of rock cocaine out of the couch, where he kept them hidden. He stuffed the drugs into his pockets and walked into the kitchen where he opened up a box of Frosted Flakes and poured two hefty bowls full. When he was finished, he poured milk into the bowl he planned to eat from, then he sat on the counter and ate. When Bobby finished his meal, he picked up the other bowl and spoon and the carton of milk and went into the bedroom. When he came into the bedroom, he put the bowl of cereal and milk on the nightstand next to the bed. Next, he dug in Mary's purse and pulled out a pen and piece of scratch paper and her car keys.

"I can't cook, Bobo," he scribbled and put the note next to the bowl. He hoped that would make her feel better. He knew he was sending her mixed messages, and it wasn't what Killa would do, but it just wasn't in him to be so hard on another human being.

Bobby put on a pair of socks with his blue house shoes and walked out of the apartment. Bobby walked into the apartment complex garage where he had Cisco's 1996 Chevy Impala SS parked next to Mary's Lexus and jeep in a vacant parking stall. Bobby shook his head; he had a lot of work to do. He took the car jacks and a tire iron out of the trunk of Mary's jeep and Lexus. He jacked up the Chevy and the Lexus and transferred the twenty-two-inch blades from the Impala to the Lexus, then he put the Lexus hubcapped tires onto the Chevy one rim at a time. It took him almost an hour and a half. Next, he removed the speaker box with two JBL fifteen-inch subwoofers inside, four six-by-nine Sony speakers, three amps, an equalizer, and a Sony CD player and radio. Bobby took the music out to the street and locked the sounds in the trunk of his car.

He returned to the parking garage and got into Mary's Lexus on the twenty-twos and headed to Los Angeles to the Park Block hood. Bobby parked the Lexus in Wicked's driveway. When he got out, he saw the pit bull in the backyard barking up a storm. "I fuckin' hate you," Bobby said as he walked to Wicked's front door.

He knocked on the screen door until Wicked's girl answered. Bobby hated her and her foul-smelling twin sister. He and almost everybody else in the hundreds had either fucked Sasha or Sonya.

"Its five a.m., nigga, what you want, Bobo?" she said from behind the screen door, closing her robe with one hand and straightening out her hair with the other.

"I ain't here for you, cuzz. Call Wicked," Bobby said impatiently.

"You ain't gonna say nothin' to me?" she asked, waiting for Bobby to say something. He didn't say anything. "Fine, nigga," she said, sticking out her tongue. "Wickeddd!" she called.

"Damn, what, cuzz?" Wicked asked, opening the screen door.

"I got to get ready for Wack Wack's party tonight. You got them dummies and the paperwork?" Bobby asked.

"Yeah, I got 'em. Come around back, I'll shoot 'em over the gate," Wicked said, disappearing into the house.

"What time is Wack Wack's party?" Sasha asked. Bobby ignored her and walked to the Lexus. He popped the trunk and pulled the car jack out. He walked to the back gate, and Wicked handed him the four dummy tires. Bobby jacked up the car and went to work changing the tires. Wicked jumped over the gate and helped Bobby change the four tires. Once the two men were finished, Wicked handed Bobby the pink slip to the Monte Carlo.

It was around six twenty in the morning when Bobby pulled in front of his protégé's Baby Bosco's mother's house on 103rd and Normandie. Bobby turned down the radio and blew the horn and waited for the boy to come out of the house. After fifteen minutes, Baby Bosco came running out of his house with cold still in his eyes as he got into the car. Bobby studied his clothing under the car's dim cabin light. Bosco sat calmly clad in a dark-blue hooded sweatshirt, black LA Gate jeans, and black Nike Cortes. His little Jheri curl shined under the car's light. He looked hood. *This little nigga is way more loced out than me. He'd probably kill me if he knew who I really am,* he thought.

"You got a heater, cuzz?" Bobby asked. Bosco lifted his shirt, revealing the butt of a rusted blue steel .38 Ruger.

"Always," he said, letting the shirt fall back in place.

Good, Bobby thought, feeling safer as he sped down Normandie to Imperial and turned into the alley behind Snappy's Market. He drove a few houses in and stopped at Lil Criptanite's house. Baby Bosco got out of the car and jumped over the back gate to get his closest roll dog. When Criptanite and Bosco got into the Lexus, Bobby pushed out of the hundreds at top speed back to Inglewood. Bobby pulled the Lexus back into the stall next to the Impala SS.

"Ya'll take the wheels off this Impala and put 'em on the Lex, and then put the Lex tires on the SS, and ya'll can have the SS. It's a jack in the trunk and one over there," Bobby said, pointing at a jack he had left in the corner. He opened the trunk of the Lexus and handed the jack to Criptanite.

"Bobo, can we go holla at Mary when we get done?" Criptanite asked. Bobby felt himself fill with anger; he probably would have slapped the shit out of the boy if he didn't suspect he was armed.

"Naw, cuzz, I ain't bring you over her foe that shit. Cuzz, don't worry about Mary," he scolded. Criptanite's face instantly balled into a frown. *Oh shit, he's going to buss on me,* Bobby thought until Criptanite's face turned into a state of pout. "Aye, Lil Crip, you heated?" Bobby asked.

"Yeah, I'm strapped like car seats, why? What's up, loc?" he asked. *Whew,* Bobby thought, thinking he had dodged a bullet.

"Oh, it ain't nothing. Them Inglewood red rag niggas been riding through, so stay on point," Bobby said, taking the four ounces out of his back pocket and gave them two ounces a piece. "Bring me $1,500, cuzz, and ya'll can keep the rest. You know that nigga Taco spot on Budlong? Cuzz is a busta. That nigga ain't no young gee. Ya'll can go serve in cuzz's spot, and he ain't gonna say shit. If that nigga say something, buss that nigga in the mouth, cuzz ain't got no thunder," Bobby advised.

"All right, cuzz," both Criptanite and Bosco agreed.

"I'm going upstairs. Ya'll can just roll when you're done," Bobby said, leaving the garage and heading upstairs to bed and lay down with Mary.

After he woke up for the second time for the day, Bobby felt much better. It seemed like Mary had sucked his soul from him and his undisturbed slumber returned his essence. Bobby pealed Mary for a hundred more dollars before he jumped into his Monte Carlo and headed to the Slauson Swap Meet. Bobby swooped into the parking lot of the swap meet, pulled under a tarp, and paid two picas to install his stolen music out of the eight hundred Mary had given him the day before. Bobby walked into the swap meet while his music was being installed; he bought a blue Hanes T-shirt and a blue Toronto Blue Jays fitted hat. That was Bobby—he's just the type of individual who could have a million dollars and he would still shop in the swap meet.

When Bobby came out the swap meet, his car was finished. Bobby got into his car and headed south on Western toward his favorite restaurant on Century, Taco Pete's. Bobby parked the Monte Carlo in the front of the hole in the wall restaurant and left the car running. He walked up to the counter to order what he always ordered: six beef tacos with cheese, a large order of French fries, and a large Coke. When his order was finished, Bobby took the grease-saturated food back to his car and got back behind the wheel. He settled in and started to eat. Bobby was just halfway done choking down his meal when he heard semiautomatic gunfire from the east of Normandie. His first instinct was to burn rubber out of the small parking lot, but he still had a greasy Taco in his hand and a hand full of fries.

After ten shots rang out, Bobby saw a white '96 Chevy Impala SS on dummies speeding westbound on Century with Baby Bosco behind the wheel. "Little niggas always getting into shit," Bobby said, shaking his head.

He finished his tacos and wiped his greasy hands on a few napkins, then he checked his navy-blue Motorola Skyway pager for the time. It was 7:16 p.m. Bobby was late for Wack Wack's homecoming party. He still did not want to go, but he promised Killa he would. *Damn, Killa always making me do shit I don't want to do,* Bobby thought.

Bobby drove east down Century and made a right turn on Normandie, noticing the yellow crime scene tape, a brown bullet-riddled 1984 Buick Regal, and two bodies covered with bloody sheets as he passed by heading south. He made another right on 104th Street and pulled into Rah Rah's driveway. Bobby blew the horn and waited until Rah Rah came out of the house and walked over to the car. Rah Rah opened the car door and slid into the passenger seat of the Monte Carlo. He handed Bobby a black .50 Desert Eagle. Bobby took the gun and let it rest in his lap. He hated guns, but he was not setting foot anywhere near Wack Wack without his blower. Even if he wasn't going to use it, Bobby hoped it would at least fend him off.

Bobby flashed back to the last time they were in the same place at the same time. Bobby had refused to fight a bigger Suicidal Gang member, so Wack Wack, better known as Monster Hands, stepped up to rumble with the bigger enemigo. Bobby sat comfortable on his top bunk as his smaller homeboy and the much bigger foe thundered toe to toe and punch for punch, until Wack Wack landed a stiff left hook to his rival's chin, knocking him unconscious. When Wack Wack came back, he challenged Bobby to a rumble. He had no desire to fight with Wack Wack, but he knew he would continue to push up on him. *What do I do?* Bobby thought in a state of panic. He saw the staff out of the corner of his left eye, and a light went off in his head—he had a brilliant idea. *How bad can it be with the staff up in here?* he asked himself as he rushed at Wack Wack, wildly swinging blindly with his head down. A few of the weak punches hit Wack Wack in the cheek and neck, but he was unfazed. He squared Bobby up and unloaded three punches, a left jab connected to Bobby's right eye, a wild right hook grazed his temple, followed by a solid quick upper cut. That landed on his chin, snapping Bobby's head back. The pressure from the blows' impact caused his knees to go limp, and his eyes closed as his unconscious frame went crashing to the dorm floor.

"So what's up with you and Wack Wack? Ya'll cool now?" Rah Rah asked, pulling Bobby back from his thoughts of Wack Wack punching his lights out.

"Fuck Wack Wack, cuzz, it's whatever," Bobby said, rubbing his chin. He turned the volume up on his favorite CD, C-Bo's *Till My Casket Drops* as he drove down Denker and 101st Street, looking for parking on the residential block. Denker was cluttered with cars. Bobby pulled the Monte Carlo into a small slot off the curb in front of CeCe's house, which had a big streetlamp overhead illuminating the pearl-white shine on the SS. The light made the Daytons look like the car was sitting on a gold mine.

Bobby was pleased with himself when he saw his older homies in the front yard of CeCe's house stalking his ride. Bobby stepped out of his car, tucking the Dessert Eagle into the waistband of his pants. He passed by his homies loitering in the front yard with Lil Rah Rah on his heels. Both men flashed the 101 gang sign as they passed by Big Money Bag, Big Criptanite, Lil OG, Big Bosco, and Big CGK, which stood for Cyco Gangsta Killa, and walked into the backyard. Bobby and Rah Rah walked into the backyard, and Lil Cold-Train made an announcement over the music from his faulty DJ position. "Tha mafuckin' killa nigga Bobo is in the mafuckin' house, Lil Rah is in the mafuckin' hooouse! All you busta niggas get the fuck ooowt!" he exclaimed drunkenly over the microphone. Several of Bobby's older and young gee homies came over to greet them both, then they returned to blazing indo and drinking while they watched the hood rats pop their booties.

Bobby was growing restless already. He and Rah Rah stood next to their homie Jon Jon, another YG.

"Where this nigga Killa at?" Bobby asked.

"Him and Wack Wack is in the house with them hos Sasha and Sonya," Jon Jon told them. Bobby's mind went to work. He knew the twins well. Killa had arranged for the two girls to send Bobby butt-naked flicks when he was in YA, and when he got out of YA, he arranged for Bobby to knock both them down, which was probably what that sucka ass nigga Wack Wack was busy doing now, he thought to himself as CeCe walked up to him and grabbed him by the balls. She leaned in close to his neck and whispered to his ear with a smile on her full man-eating lips, "Bobo, baby, let's go in the house. I got a surprise for you."

Bobby looked at her like she was crazy. He had already had CeCe, and he didn't want anything her thick ass was giving, surprise or not. He looked over CeCe's shoulder, spotting Mya, a little light-skinned number from down the block he had seen around. "Beat it, bitch," he said, pushing CeCe off him. "Go suck Killa or Wack's dick, bitch, you're old news." He left her dumbfounded as he walked off and plopped down on the couch next to Mya.

"What's crackin', ma?" he said, going right into his spiel. "Where you going tonight, cuzz I can see you rollin' with a young gee."

"Is that right?" she said, liking Bobby's cockiness.

"Yeah, that's right. You know you lookin' good, and I want that and you want a nigga too, so let's cut the shenanigans," he said, watching Mya light up and start to blush.

"You just too much," she said, knowing she would be going with him. Bobby was about to respond when he saw Baby Bosco and Lil Criptanite come running into the backyard straight at him and Mya on the couch.

"Bobo, cuzz, we got in a big shootout with the homies on Century," Bosco said.

"Damn, cuzz, little niggas fuckin' up my spit," he said to Mya, who laughed. "What happened, cuzz?"

"We went over to Taco's spot and started slangin' like you said. Cuzz come out trippin' like we shortstopping his work. Cuzz got into an argument with Baby Bosco, and Bosco called cuzz out on a rumble and faded cuzz. We jumped in the SS and stabbed out to the big doughnut drive-through. We ordering some doughnuts from Kendal's, and the nigga Taco pulled up at the Taco Bell in his Regal. He was with the homie Lil Layso next to us. That nigga told Layso to get out and fade Bosco, so when cuzz got out the car, I got out the car and shot cuzz three times, then I ran up on the Regal and shot that muthafucka six or seven times. Then we rolled to my cuzzin's house in Inglewood," Lil Criptanite narrated.

Damn, I caused this. This was my doing, Bobby thought as he turned around and grabbed hold of Mya's hand, who sat on the couch, ear hustling the conversation between himself, Bosco, and Criptanite. "You comin' wit me or what?" he asked as he saw a drunken Wack Wack stagger out of CeCe's house into the backyard with Killa, Sasha, and Sonya.

"Yeah, I'll come. Where we going?" she asked pulling, Bobby's hand for support as she got back to her feet. Bobby tried to speed by Killa and Wack Wack. *At least he came. He had his own business to tend to now,* he thought.

"Bobo, west crackin', cuzz?" Killa said as Bobby zoomed by. *Damn*, Bobby thought, turning around to face Killa and Wack Wack. Killa gave Bobby a half hug and shook his hand. Bobby extended his hand to Wack Wack.

"What's crackin', cuzz?" he said in greeting.

Wack Wack just looked down at Bobby's hand with a smirk on his face. "Nigga, don't say nothing to me," he said.

Killa stepped between both of his homeboys, keeping them separated. "Wack Wack, cuzz, you trippin' crip," Killa said, trying to keep the peace.

"Naw, cuzz, I'm tellin' you, this nigga is a hook after you left the Y. This scary-ass nigga Bobby lost focus." Wack Wack started to rant and concentrated on his physical. To Bobby, he looked the same. He was still short, and his face was still clean-shaven except for a thin mustache. He wore a black T-shirt, khakis, and Nike Cortez. Bobby could see the twenty-inch-thick arms straining against the cheap fabric of Wack Wack's shirt and knew he did not want any part of a rumble with him. When he came out of his trance sizing him up, he looked at the faces of Lil Criptanite, Baby Bosco, and Mya, who all looked shocked listening to Wack Wack scream about his behavior in YA.

It was all starting to set into Bobby. His stripes were on the line, and as scared of Wack Wack as he was, he could not allow him to wipe away the stripes he had shamed for. He had to stop Wack Wack before he exposed too much. Bobby became a force of action without thought. "Bitch ass nigga, you lying! I rushed yo punk ass in YA on Teennn One Block Crip," he screamed, pulling the Desert Eagle from the front of his waistband, aimin' it across Killa in Wack Wack's direction. *This ought to scare him enough 'cause I don't wanna shoot*, Bobby started to think, until his inner thoughts were interrupted by Wack Wack, who had pulled a chrome .38 snub nose revolver out of his pants, which Killa had given him earlier in the day. Bobby panicked as he did all those years ago when he ran over Haunchie Bear. He pulled the trigger three times, firing wildly. Wack Wack got off two shots in Bobby's direction as both he and Killa dove out the way of the Desert Eagle rounds. Baby Bosco and Lil Criptanite pulled out their guns and started shooting at Wack Wack. Wack Wack dropped his pistol and ran into the house for cover.

Bobby grabbed Mya's hand and ran out the backyard to the SS. Bosco and Criptanite took off after him to the front yard. Sasha was walking out of the backyard as they got into the Chevy Impala. Criptanite started the car and rolled down the windows.

"Aye, Sasha, cuzz, come here," he called her over to the car. She was faded out of her mind, and when she walked to the car, Bosco could smell the liquor she had consumed coming out of her pores. "Aye, Sasha, get in," Bosco said.

"Naw, boy, I gotta find my sister and get home. That nigga Wicked be trippin'," she said.

They saw Bobby start up his car and star to pull off. "We'll drop you off, hurry up and get in," Criptanite said.

"All right," Sasha said and got into the back seat of the car and closed the door. Criptanite put the car in gear and drove off after Bobby and Mya.

5

USING STRIPES

Bobby woke up in the small bed inside the Carpet Inn Motel on Century and Fig. Mya was snuggled up in the bed next to him still asleep. He studied her as she slept. She may have been the most beautiful woman he had ever seen, he thought, as he ran his eyes down what he could see of her body exposed from the bed's covers. She had large C-cup breasts, a small waist, wide hips, and a big, firm butt. She was a small woman, but she was really put together. Bobby looked at her face. Most of the makeup she wore the night before had come off while sweating during their sexual romps throughout the night, and still her face was angelic. She had a small forehead with thin brown eyebrows and soft brown eyes. She had a small nose, which accentuated her cheekbones and her pouty full lips. Mya opened her eyes and looked confused as Bobby looked her over. He leaned in and gave her a long, deep kiss on the lips, his thoughts drifting back to the events from Wack Wack's homecoming. After the shootout in CeCe's backyard, Bobby and Mya slid into his Super Sport and took off, then he slowed down for Baby Bosco and Lil Criptanite to get into the Impala and follow behind him. He saw his two TGs pick up Sasha and followed behind him to Normandie. Then they flew down Century to the Carpet Inn Motel. He got two rooms for the night, one for him and Mya and one for the boys and Sasha. He said he would see them in the morning and walked into the room with Mya.

Bobby withdrew from the kiss and looked Mya in the eyes as his conscience took on another reason to feel like shit. He wondered if she could see the guilt in his eyes, but she couldn't. *Damn, I know this shit ain't right,* he thought, feeling like he was betraying what he and Mary had for a moment, but it was only for a moment, as he felt Mya's hands on his Johnson. She was the total package—sexy, beautiful, and gangsta; after all, she did just witness him shoot at a man in a shootout last night, and now here she was in bed with him. *Naw, she is just too good to be true. I would have to make it up to Mary some other time,* he thought as he positioned himself on top of Mya and started to kiss her. *Damn, I'm making love to this broad,* Bobby said to himself, somewhat amazed at how much he was into Mya.

After his morning sexcapade, Bobby got out of bed and headed for the room the two teens and Sasha were staying in. He turned the door handle and opened the door without knocking. What he saw made him wish he had knocked. Both Sasha and Criptanite were both nude on top of the bed. Sasha was on all fours, and Criptanite was positioned behind her, pumping in her from the back. Neither of them stopped as Bobby came into the room, which made him view her like he had never done before. Bobby had never liked Sasha. He even went as far as selling her half-nude flicks in YA. Sasha was not his type. She was average looking with a so-so face, small breasts, and an ass that looked like she had two bowling balls under her kin. She wore a long weave and a ton of makeup, but what Bobby hated most was her vaginal odor, like her sister, but not as bad.

Bosco walked out of the bathroom and saw Bobby at the front door. He strolled across the motel. "Aye, cuzz, I need to holla at you," Bobby said, looking back at the scene on the bed inside. Once they were outside and alone, Bobby put his arm around Bosco's shoulder, pulling him under his wing. This kid had proven without a doubt that he was a loyal soldier in Bobby's army.

"Aye, cuzz, you should change yo name. Fuck them Bosco niggas, loc. You under me now, cuzz. Fuck 'em, you under a true young gee," Bobby said.

Baby Bosco's face lit up as he nodded, accepting the new moniker. "I want ya'll to drop Sasha off and meet me in the Park hood. Do not go to the park and the hood! Stay out the hood until I meet ya'll there in the Park."

"All right, cuzz," the newly dubbed Lil Bobo agreed. Bobby went back to his room to get Mya to take her home. When Bobby got on Ninety-Ninth Street and Budlong, he parked in front of Mya's house. He saw a few of the Cyco Gangsta Crips standing out in front of Red's liquor store, looking at him like he was crazy for being in their hood. His fear and paranoia started to get the best of him. He had always been scared shitless of the Cyco Gangsta's after he mowed down Big Haunchie, but he'd risk it for Mya.

"I thought you lived in the hood," he said as she got out the car.

"My granny stay in yo hood, that's why I'm over there," she said.

Bobby took a quick look over his shoulder at the hoods at the store. "I'll call you later tonight," he said and slammed his foot down on the car's gas pedal, burning rubber off Budlong. As Bobby pushed top speed through Los Angeles traffic, his worry shifted to Wack Wack and Killa. *What would they do next? Did Killa think they were shooting at him too? Would Killa really kill me? Fuck, I ain't going to the hood no more,* he thought as he pulled into the parking garage of his Inglewood apartment complex. He parked next to Mary's Lexus. Her jeep was parked out on the street. When he walked into the apartment, Mary was sitting at the dining table entertaining a few of her girlfriends. Mary's eyes lit up when she saw Bobby come in.

"Oh hi, Bobby, I was just telling my friends about you," she said, and her friends all started to laugh and giggle.

"Aye, Mary, I need to talk to you in the room," he said, pulling her by the elbow and leading her into the bedroom. Bobby closed the door and slammed Mary against it. He started to kiss her, running his hands under her dress and pulling down her panties. He took the Desert Eagle from his waist and tossed it on to the bed. He undid his pants and let them fall to his ankles.

"Bobby, wait, my friends," Mary said, pulling her lips from his.

"So what!" he said, grabbing both of Mary's legs on either side of him and lifting her up against the door.

"Bobby, we shouldn't," Mary said, hoping Bobby would ignore her modest plea.

"This is what I need," Bobby said, easing himself into Mary's center. Mary thrashed about on the door, screaming Bobby's name, putting on a show for her unattractive friends that never got any at home. Just as Bobby pulled away from her, she smelled the scent of another woman.

"Bobby, you are fucking nasty. Get your hands off me!" she shouted.

"What? What are you trippin' for, cuzz?" Bobby asked confused.

"You been with another bitch. How you go stick your dirty dick in me? You ain't even showered. You fuckin' smell like sex," Mary said, putting on her panties and opening up the door to walk out the room.

"Sex? What sex? That's yo sex you smellin'! Fuck what you goin' through, Mary. I ain't fuck nobody but you!" he screamed after her as she walked out the room. Bobby felt like shit when he took his shower for cheating on Mary. He felt even worst about being caught. When he got out of the shower, he got dressed in a blue Fubu jersey and a pair of blue DKNY denim shorts and blue-and-white nylon Nike Cortez. He strolled into the living room and almost jumped out of his skin when he saw Killa sitting on the couch with his feet on the coffee table.

"Awe, Killa, what's up?" Bobby asked, trying to regain his composure at the sight of who he believed was Satan himself in his living room.

"Aye, loc, cuzz, that shit you pulled was fucked up," Killa said.

What, Mr. Shoot-and-Rob-Any-Homie-You-Want-To, how the fuck dare you? Bobby thought. "Killa, I always support you when you make blackout moves, so support me cuzz. Fuck Wack Wack, cuzz!" Bobby didn't know how Killa would respond. He'd seen his wrath in the past, but he himself had never stood up to him. Killa stood up from the couch and walked over to Bobby until they stood face-to-face.

"Cuzz, ya'll hit like foe homeboys and the big home girl Donna Loc. You my nigga, cuzz, but them little niggas gotta go!" Killa screamed.

Bobby knew he should do the right thing. He knew he should stand up for the boys. He knew he should have a spine, but instead he said, "I'll take you to them little niggas, cuzz."

"All right, cool, let's roll," Killa said as Mary walked into the apartment, coming back from walking her last friend to her car. Killa grabbed Mary around the waist, pulling her against him. "I'm stressed out, girl. Hook ya boy up with some of that bomb dome action you got," Killa said.

Mary gave a light struggle, looking to Bobby for approval. "It-it-it's up to Bobo," she whimpered.

Killa's face contorted into a frown. "Bitch, stop playin'," he said, tightening his grip even tighter.

She looked for Bobby to make a decision or help her. "Bo-Bo-Bobo," she stuttered.

"Naw, Killa, cuzz, you doing too much, loc," Bobby said, even surprising himself with the words that left his lips.

Killa pushed Mary to the ground. "Nigga, what? I run this bitch, nigga. I gave you this ho!" Killa screamed.

It is time to man up now. If Killa went for my first aggressive gestures, maybe he would just back down now, Bobby thought. "I wouldn't give a fuck, nigga. She my bitch now, cuzz. This is my muthafuckin' house!" Bobby screamed.

Killa closed the distance between himself and Bobby. In a flash, the last thing Bobby saw was Killa's red eyes, then he felt a hard right hook connect with the left side of his chin, knocking him down onto his hands and knees.

I wasn't even willing to ride for my young TGs, now I am the victim of Killa's assault over a punk bitch, Bobby thought through a haze of stars. He felt Killa's hands under his armpits, lifting him back to his feet. He heard Mary screaming off to the side of the room somewhere. *Stupid bitch,* he thought.

Killa struck Bobby in the jaw with another hook, then another. Bobby put his head down and started to swing wildly at Killa, who blocked or stepped out of the way of the uneducated fists Bobby threw. Killa put his left hand on top of Bobby's head and measured him for the right blow. Killa stuck a stiff upper cut into Bobby's left eye and a left hook to the right side of his temple, sending Bobby falling backward into the coffee table. Shattered wood and wood chips flew all over the living room floor. Bobby tried to get up off his back into a sitting position, but Killa kicked him in the face, knocking him back down. Killa stood over him and started to stomp down on his head, neck, arms, and chest. Blood leaked profusely from the deep cuts and gash in Bobby's face and upper torso.

Oh my god, Killa is going to stomp me to death if I don't do something, he thought. "Help, Mary! Heellpp! Hit him with somethin'!" Bobby screamed.

Mary stopped screaming and picked up the broken coffee table leg and struck Killa hard across the back, snapping the stick in half. Killa stumbled forward from the blow, then he regained his footing and spun his murderous rage on Mary, punching her in the face and the stomach. After the beating he took, Bobby felt as though he didn't have anything left in him. The only thing driving him to his feet and stumbling into the bedroom was the thought that Killa would not stop until both he and Mary were dead.

Bobby grabbed the .50 semiautomatic he had gotten from Lil Rah Ra off the bed, where he had tossed it earlier. *Maybe he'll stop when he sees the gun. He'll stop,* Bobby thought, wiping the flowing blood from his eyes. He walked into the living room on unsteady legs. Killa was still beating Mary, stomping and kicking her in the face and ribs.

"Killa, stop, nigga," Bobby said, pointing the gun at Killa's back. He stopped kicking Mary and turned around to look at Bobby.

"Nigga, you pullin' a gun on me, cuzz?" Killa said.

Bobby frowned. "K, cuzz, you trippin', loc. Just roll out, cuzz," Bobby said, tightening his grip on the large butt of the Desert Eagle. Killa lunged across the short distance between himself and Bobby. When his hands went around the gun, Bobby panicked and squeezed the gun's trigger one time, sending a round from the gun into Killa's forehead, snapping back his neck. Killa's body went limp as the bullet exited the back of his skull, and he collapsed to the floor of the apartment.

Mary screamed at the top of her lungs. "Aaaah! Bobby, no!" she cried. "You killed him! Noooo!" she said, putting her bloody face in her hands.

Damn, maybe I should kill her too, he thought. *What the fuck am I saying? I got to get the fuck out of here.* "Mary, I'm sorry, girl, I'm sorry for everything," Bobby said, running out of the apartment with blood dripping from his face and the pistol hanging from his hand.

Bobby got into his SS, his blood staining the interior. He pulled the keys from his pocket, shoved the key in the car's ignition, and started the car. He dropped the gun into his lap, shifted the car into gear, reversed out of the parking stall, put the car in drive, and smashed out of the parking garage. He had to get out of Los Angeles, and he had to get out fast.

"Bobby Lee, you are sentenced to life in state prison," Bobby heard the voice of the white judge that sent him to YA. Bobby shook his head and tried to refocus on the road. He pulled over his car on Crenshaw and Manchester to get himself together. Bobby looked at himself in the side-view mirror. His left eyebrow was split open with a hard knot underneath it. The bleeding had formed a clot and stopped the blood flow. His bottom lip had a deep gash in it from his own teeth; his nose was swollen, and he had a slug under his right eye. His forearms were also sore, cut, and swollen. "Damn, Killa, how you do ya boy like that? I gotta get out of here before I get picked up by the police. I'm not doing life, cuzz, but I need money. Them little niggas should have my dope money," he said to himself.

Bobby pulled up to Wicked's house on 109th Street and blew the horn. He wouldn't dare get out and be seen by the Parks in his condition, mental and physical. He saw the white Impala SS on Wicked's front lawn.

Lil Bobo leaned into the driver-side window and looked at Bobby's face. "What the fuck happened to you, cuzz?" Lil Criptanite asked.

"I just smoked that scary-ass nigga Killa. Cuzz tried to see me over that bitch, Mary, on some hater shit," Bobby lied. The two boys looked at Bobby in awe because he just killed a legend, a true warrior. "Yeah though, cuzz, I need that dope money," Bobby said, snapping the boys back into reality from their trance.

"Here, cuzz," Lil Bobo said, handing Bobby a fistful of dollar bills.

Lil Criptanite dug the money from his pocket and handed it through the window. "We couldn't slang it all, but that's what we got," he said.

Damn, it's still not enough, I need more, Bobby thought as he saw Wack Wack, Big Money, and Big Time Bomb roll up and park across the street in Time Bomb's six tray. Wack Wack was the car's driver. Bobby saw him reach under the seat as he hit a switch, dropping the Chevy Impala to the ground on all four wheels like a pancake.

"Aye, Bobo, there go that nigga Wack Wack," Criptanite said.

"Yeah, I see him," Bobby said.

6

LIFE OR DEATH

Bobby strained his neck to try to get a better look at Wack Wack in the low-low. Sonya walked out of her mother's house and walked over to the passenger-side window of the gold lowrider.

"Hey, Wackie, my sister is still in there asleep. That bitch came back about three hours ago drunk, but I can roll with ya'll by myself," she said, counting the three men in the car. She could, without a doubt, handle all three of the men herself. Sonya's words seemed to fall on deaf ears as Wack Wack turned around in the front seat to look back at Money.

"Cuzz, ya'll kick back, I'm about to chip these niggas," he said, putting the TEC-9 he had pulled from under the seat on his lap.

"Hold up, cuzz!" Time Bomb protested.

Sonya's eyes got big as she saw the murderous weapon. "Not in front of my house, Wack, un-unh," she said.

"What? Them niggas shot at me. Bomb, fuck that! Bitch, shut the fuck up. This Crip business, stupid-ass ho," he said, opening the car door and stepping out of the Chevy with the TEC-9 behind his back.

"Cuzz getting out, Bobo, you want us to blaze this nigga or what?" Lil Criptanite asked.

Bobby knew he should just cut his losses and drive off. What if the police hit the corner? He was tempted to go, but the sight of Wack Wack's frown made him change his mind. His rage and hatred overpowered his fear. This shit was all over Wack Wack; Killa had only beaten him to a bloody pulp because he came to defend Wack Wack. *Fuck that,* he thought.

"You got yo straps, little niggas?" he asked his little homeboys.

"Got mine!" Lil Criptanite said. Lil Bobo shook his head no. Bobby handed Lil Bobo the Desert Eagle. "Kill that muthafucka right now—all them fools!" he demanded.

Criptanite pulled a chrome .380 from his waistband, backed away from the car, and turned around, shooting just as Wack Wack stepped away from the lowrider. The gun's explosion sounded off in the still of the residential neighborhood. Wack Wack was caught off guard; he was outdrawn. Lil Bobo pulled up next to Criptanite and started shooting the big Desert Eagle. Wack Wack shot off four rounds toward the boys. One of the bullets tore into the front of the fiberglass front fender of Bobby's Monte Carlo; the other three bullets whizzed by the boys and slammed into the side of Wicked's house. Sonya pushed away from the car when the shooting started. She ran back into her house to call the police while Time Bomb and Money ducked down in the lowrider for cover.

Wack Wack turned around to run back to the car, spraying the TEC-9 blindly with his back toward Criptanite and Lil Bobo. Lil Criptanite took aim and squeezed off six more rounds into Wack Wack's back. The bullets exploded into his chest and lungs. Wack Wack dropped the TEC-9 to the ground and felt for the newly made holes in his chest leaking blood. The blood started to well up in his throat and run out of his mouth as he leaned up against the bullet-riddled lowrider.

"What you waitin' on? Shoot that busta down," Bobby directed.

Lil Bobo aimed the Desert Eagle at Wack Wack's back and pulled the trigger, putting two more slugs into his bleeding frame. Wack Wack fell backward to the street, spitting up blood. He felt a numbing pain in his legs; his chest felt like it was on fire from the bullets and bullet holes in his upper torso.

Lil Criptanite walked over to the dying man and held the gun over his face and shot two more rounds into his face, putting him out of his misery. Criptanite picked up the TEC-9 off the street and sprayed the remaining rounds of the TEC into Time Bomb's lowrider. The bullets ripped through the steel sheet metal and went into both Time Bomb and Big Money. Big Money took a slug to the head, killing him instantly; Time Bomb took two bullets to the back as he tried to crawl out of the car. He made it out of the car onto the sidewalk. Lil Bobo ran around the car and executed his big homeboy with two bullets out of the big Desert Eagle to the back of his brain.

Damn. Not long ago, I'd given these little niggas up to Killa, and if he was alive now, they'd be the ones executed in front of Sonya and Sasha's house. I gotta get out of here. I've pulled my last move, he thought. "Bobby Lee!" he heard the judge's voice call out to him.

"Noooo!" he screamed, his head spinning from the mild concussion he had suffered at the feet of Killa. "Awwe shit," Bobby moaned, starting up the Monte Carlo SS, putting the car in gear, and speeding off in top speed toward Denker, leaving Lil Bobo and Lil Criptanite in the street. Bobby hooked a right turn on 101st Street. *I need some more money,* he thought, turning into his YG homeboy G Ball's driveway. Bobby stabilized himself before he got out of the car with the motor still running. He stumbled to the front door and pounded on it as if his life depended on it.

"G Ball! Baaall! G Ball!" he shouted until G Ball answered the front door. "G Ball, cuzz, I need some chips, cuzz. The pigs is lookin' for me," he pleaded.

G Ball smoked him over skeptically. "What happened to you, cuzz?" he asked, genuinely concerned. The concern on G Ball's face made Bobby realize he was acting too dramatic; his fear was getting the best of him, so he tried to bring it down a bit and act like a man. After all, he was still Bobo loc—the number 2 killer under Killa loc from Concrete Block in everyone else's mind.

"I had to chip that bitch-ass nigga Killa at Mary's house. Nigga, the pigs gonna be in the hood any minute. I need some money to run, loc." Bobby knew G Ball still had ill feelings toward Killa for pulling the blower on him in the backyard, so he figured G Ball would be happy Killa was dead and willing to help out.

"That's what that foul nigga get. I got like $500 foe you in the tilt, just hold up a minute while I get it," G Ball said, patting his pockets as he walked into the house. Bobby counted the money he had gotten from Lil Bobo and Lil Criptanite. It was only $825. The $500 from G Ball would be enough for him to get on to Texas and set up a new life for himself with his aunt Barbara Lee.

Yeah, that's what I'll do, he thought. As he waited, a sherbet orange–candy painted 1984 Chevy wagon on seventeen-inch gold Daytons and low-profile tires with 2 Pac's "All Eyes on Me" full blast came pulling up. The Malibu pulled into the driveway behind Bobby's Monte Carlo, blocking him in. Bobby's head started to spin from the throbbing music. He saw five stars before his eyes, then the judge's face, and pictured hearing his voice. "Bobby Lee, you will serve life in the state prison. Bobby Lee, Bobby Lee, life, life, life."

Bobby put his hands to his temples to try to block out the sounds of the music and the judge. The pain became so unbearable he closed his eyes. When Bobby opened his eyes, G Ball was coming out of his house. He handed Bobby the $500. Two men got out of the Malibu and made their way over to the front porch. As they got closer, Bobby recognized the two men as Big Cisco and his baby brother, the up-and-coming TG Lil Cisco.

Damn, I hope these niggas don't trip, he thought, feeling his waist for the Desert Eagle Lil Rah Rah had given him the night before. Then it hit him, he was unarmed. He had given his piece to his little homeboy's to shoot Wack Wack.

Fuck! My day just keeps getting worse and worse, he thought as his whole face started to throb.

"Bobo, what's up, cuzz? I been lookin' for you and that nigga Killa," Cisco said as he walked onto the front porch, followed by his baby brother, sizing Bobby up.

"Damn, cuzz, what happened to your face?" he asked.

"I ain't got time, Cisco, cuzz," Bobby said, trying to push past Cisco, who stopped him short with a hand to his chest.

"Hold up, fool, you niggas jacked me, and you think I'm a let you just walk up outta here? You got the game fucked up," Cisco said, pulling a .357 Magnum out of the front of his pants.

This can't be happening to me—not now. Bobby thought he was losing his grip. *I have got to try something.* He turned slightly so that he could face both Cisco and his little brother. "Nigga, what? You know me, muthafucka. I just smoked Killa and that nigga Wack Wack. So what you think I'm a do to you, nigga? I'm a muthafuckin young gee. I'm Bobo, nigga, me! Not you! How you gonna pull steel on a killa?" Bobby ranted, betting it all on one roll, hoping it wouldn't be his last. His charade worked wonders on Big Cisco. He was actually contemplating lowering the .357 he pulled on Bobby, but Lil Cisco remained unfazed.

"Cuzz, you niggas robbed my brother. I don't give a fuck who you are, nigga, this crip! Take all that shit off, or I'm dumpin' nigga that's on my dead Mama!" he said, pulling a .45 from the small of his back and pointed it at Bobby's face.

Bobby looked down the barrel of the .45 and saw a cemetery. He had rolled snake eyes and crapped out, but this was his life, and he wasn't going to just give it up. His fear of jail and death would not allow it.

"Hold up, cuzz, we all homies. Cisco, ya'll trippin'," G Ball said. His words broke Lil Cisco's concentration long enough for Bobby to hurl himself into the frail teenager, knocking him to the ground. He hopped over him and ran toward G Ball's backyard. He heard three loud explosions behind him from Lil Cisco's .45 as he shot wildly, tryin' to get back to his feet. Two of the bullets slammed into the garage and another hit the roof of G Ball's 1985 K-5 Chevy Blazer, barely missing his head.

Bobby ran to the fence in G Ball's backyard and jumped to the top of the chain-link fence. He used his upper-body strength to vault over the gate into the alley on the other side. Bobby's foot landed in a slick puddle of oil, causing him to slip and fall, landing on the back of his head. Bobby used the gate to help pull himself back to his feet. He heard the white judge's voice bouncing around in his head. "Bobby Lee, you are going to jail, you have life in prison."

"Nooo! Get out of my head!" he screamed. "Leave me alone."

Lil Criptanite turned the 1996 Chevy Impala down the alley and headed toward Bobby. He stopped the car short, and the two boys got out of the car. "Bobo, what's up, cuzz?" Lil Bobo asked.

Bobby's vision was distorted in his mind. He saw a white Chevy Caprice instead of the SS Impala. Instead of seeing Lil Criptanite and Lil Bobo, he saw the judge and a Lennox Sheriff exit the car he believed to be a police vehicle.

"I ain't going to jail!" Bobby screamed. Lil Criptanite and Lil Bobo both looked at each other, confused. Bobby turned around and jumped back over the gate into the back of G Ball's yard, forgetting why he had jumped the gate in the first place. Lil Criptanite and Lil Bobo got back into the Impala and took off down the alley. Bobby leaned against the fence for support to stay on his feet; his head continued to spin, and he started to have a hard time breathing.

Fuck, what am I going to do? Bobby thought, clutching his chest.

Lil Cisco came running down the driveway into the backyard, where he found Bobby leaning against the back gate. "Yeah, what now, nigga? Fuck yo life!" he said, standing in front of Bobby at blank range. He aimed the big .45 at Bobby's chest and squeezed off six rounds. The bullets hit him in the chest and stomach, ripping through his abdomen and tearing into his intestines. Two of the rounds blew through his lungs and his right ribs. Bobby didn't stand a chance surviving the bullets he just taken. He fell to the ground, holding his stomach from the burning, searing pain the hot bullets caused. Lil Cisco turned around, tucking the .45 back down the front of his pants and ran back down the driveway to the front yard.

Bobby laid down in a pool of his own blood. He heard the throbbing sounds of 2 Pac blasting out of the speakers of the Malibu as the two brothers started up the car and fled the scene. Bobby could hear sirens in the distance, but he knew neither the police nor the paramedics were coming to rescue him. His senses started to intensify. He could smell the grass and dirt from across the yard. Tears started to stream out of Bobby's eyes as he realized he was a dead man.

"I'm not going to make it. Oh, Lord God, please help me," he pleaded as a sharp pain shot up into his chest. "Aaah! Nooo!" he screamed out to the heavens. "Fuck it, cuzz, I'm ready to go," he said, still faking as he felt what seemed like a fist gripping around his heart. He started to foam at the mouth and seize, then he went still.

After Bobby's death, Mary paid for his funeral at the Inglewood Cemetery. Both Killa and Wack Wack were cremated weeks after the funeral. Mary learned that she had contracted herpes from Bobby, who contracted STD from having unprotected sex with Mya. She took the negative experiences of having Killa and Bobby in her life and created her own business and life. She also underwent reconstructive plastic surgery on her face.

Lil Criptanite got twenty-five years in Texas for a bank robbery two years after Bobby's murder. When G Ball was arrested in a drug deal gone bad, he cracked under the pressure and helped close the case of the murder investigations on Wack Wack, Big Money, and Time

Bomb. He also implicated Lil Criptanite in the murders of Taco and Layso. Lil Criptanite was extradited back to stand trial in California for five murders and given the death penalty.

Lil Bobo was living life to the fullest. After Bobby's death, he started to rob banks with Lil Criptanite. He barely made it out of Texas with the money when Criptanite was arrested. By the time G Ball started to talk, he was already established as a major hood figure and a well-respected killer. Everything was going his way until he saw Lil Cisco getting gas at the Circle K gas station on Normandie and Century. He walked up and blew Lil Cisco's brains all over the trunk of his Regal, all under watchful eye of the gas station surveillance cameras. Lil Bobo went on the run to Seattle, Washington.

The same things went on in the Concrete Block Crip hood with Killa and the rest of the real killers out of the neighborhood. The Concretes went back to being shot up by the Suicidals and the Cyco Gangstas, and under the new leadership of Big Cisco, the cycle of faking for stripes continued.

SUNSET
ROMEO CONWAY

IN TOO DEEP

"So you got the goods or what, dog?" Kenny asked the dark-skinned six-foot man standing before him dressed in his flashy clothes and long platinum chains hanging down to his waist. Following the chain led Kenny's probing eyes to rest on the butt of a .44 semiautomatic Desert Eagle, which protruded over the top of his waistband for all to see.

"Yeah, dog, I got it. How ya'll wanna do this?" the flashy hood answered, looking over Kenny's short, white, balding business partner he had brought along for the deal.

"We'll do it just like we discussed, Yo Yo baby, ain't nothing changed," Kenny said with a smile.

Yo Yo realized he didn't like Kenny's smile. *There's something unsettling about him and that smile,* he thought. He took in the rest of Kenny's appearance in the dark alley, illuminated only by the car and truck lights of his own Cadillac STS and Kenny's Range Rover. Kenny was a big man at six-foot-one, 220 pounds of solid muscle. He had menacing piercing black eyes that seemed to look straight through you. His nose was wide and twisted on the bridge. He had bushy eyebrows, and he kept his facial hair neatly trimmed in a full beard. His hair was freshly braided in nine cornrows straight to the back with red rubber bands on the tips. Kenny's face was still twisted in his grotesque smile when Yo Yo signaled for his two armed henchmen to bring the two briefcases from the trunk of the car to where they were. Kenny looked around the alley to make sure they were alone still; they were, so he signaled his partner to retrieve the two kilograms from the back seat of the Range Rover. John put two bricks of cocaine on the hood of the black truck while Yo Yo's goons brought over the two briefcases and set them next to where John had sat the cocaine.

"It's all there, my nigga, you know how Big K-Dog do!" Kenny said, looking at the face of the up-and-coming drug lord. Kenny could sense uneasy feeling.

"All right, K-Dog, let me check it out for quality though," Yo Yo said, walking over to the hood of the truck. Kenny followed behind him to observe him check the merchandise over. Yo Yo picked up the closest package to him and pealed back the plastic and tape that the cocaine was sealed in. John watched both ends of the alley as cars drove by. He checked his watch as though he were waiting on something. He brought his attention back to Kenny, who was busy watching Yo Yo try the cocaine powder. A yellow taxi turned into the far end of the alley and sped toward the two parked vehicles, drawing the attention of the five men in the alley doing the drug deal. The taxi pulled to a stop behind the Cadillac STS and started to blow the horn.

"What the fuck is that, bruh?" Kenny asked surprised.

Blinded by his own greed, Yo Yo refocused on the cocaine in his grasp. "I don't know, Dog! Bozack, go check that shit out blood," he said, taking his pinky finger covered in cocaine and touched it to his tongue.

Bozack walked around the Cadillac toward the taxi when he reached the driver's side of the car, he looked into the car window. The taxi driver was a black man with a thick mustache and blue Dodgers hat. It was all he could see under the dimly lit conditions of the alley. He knocked on the cab window. The driver rolled down the glass window. "Put that shit in reverse and take it around ba—"

Before Bozack could finish his sentence, two rounds jumped out of a .38 revolver the cab driver had in his lap. The two bullets struck their mark. The first bullet tore through Bozack's forehead and lodged in his brain. The second slug ripped through his left eye and burst out the back of his skull, snapping his head back and sending his lifeless body slamming up against a large dumpster. Bozack's body fell to the ground and started its death dance.

After hearing the two gunshots that took Bozack's life, John snatched a .357 Magnum from the front of his waistband with lightning speed and pumped four rounds from point-blank range into Yo Yo's other stooge, blowing the dying man against the Cadillac hood before he even knew what had hit him.

"What the fuck, blood?" Yo Yo screamed.

Kenny grabbed the Desert Eagle out of Yo Yo's waistband with his left hand while he struck him with a combined elbow-forearm blow in one swift motion. The blow took Yo Yo by surprise, breaking his nose and sending him crashing to the ground in the alley.

"Damn, blood, what the fuck is this shit, K-Dog?" he mumbled, tending to his right swollen eye. The cab driver joined the other three surviving men between the Cadillac and Range Rover with a roll of tape in his hands.

"Tape this nigga up, cuzz," Kenny said, playing with Yo Yo's mind, whose eyes got wide.

Darryl Johnson, the cab driver, went to work binding the injured man's hands at the wrist behind his back with the thick silver duct tape. Once Yo Yo was bound, Darryl and John lifted him up off the ground and escorted him to the back of the cab, put him into the back seat of the car, and locked him in. Kenny pushed the fake kilograms of cocaine off the hood of the truck into the alley and grabbed the two briefcases with the twenty-seven thousand Yo Yo had planned on paying for the two kilos of fake cocaine. He put the two cases into the back seat of the Range Rover while John and Darryl loaded the two dead bodies of Yo Yo's goons into the Cadillac STS.

When the men were loaded into the driver's seat and passenger seat of the Cadillac, John slid into the back seat next to Yo Yo and put the .357 up against the side of his head.

"Look, we are going to take you to your house where you keep your dope, and you are going to give it to us or we will kill you like we killed your homeboys. This is not a game!" John said sternly.

"Who are ya'll, man? Crips? Man, don't kill me, just don't melt me," Yo Yo pleaded.

John shook his head. "No, we are professionals," he said. Kenny pulled his Range Rover to a stop behind the taxicab in front of Yo Yo's townhouse.

Yo Yo had a large townhouse he shared with his wife on the west side of Sunset. There was a big candy-apple red Cadillac Escalade on twenty-two-inch chrome rims in the driveway. He looked up into the starlit night sky as John and Darryl handled Yo Yo from the back of the cab and dragged him down the walkway to his front door. Kenny followed behind the three men, making sure no one saw the trio.

"Where's the keys?" Darryl asked Yo Yo.

"In my right front pocket, dog," he said. Darryl dug the keys out of his pocket and tried them on the door until the lock unlatched. The four men walked into the house and shut the front door behind them. Darryl forced Yo Yo down onto the red leather couch in the middle of the living room. Kenny looked around the house, studying the decor. The house was covered with red carpet and red furnishings; all the walls were white.

"Not bad, kid," Kenny said about the townhouse.

"Let's get this shit done and get out of here," John said, putting his pistol against Yo Yo's temple. "We already told you the scoop, now take us to the money."

Yo Yo looked up from the couch at the overweight Jewish man with contempt in his eyes. "Man, dog, you know what? I kinda changed my mind. Ya'll just gotta do what ya'll gotta do. If ya'll gonna beat me, beat me. If ya'll gonna kill me, then kill me. Fuck ya'll blood," Yo Yo said defiantly.

"What?" John screamed and slapped Yo Yo hard across the face with the side of the big Magnum, sending blood flying across the couch from his mouth and already broken nose.

"Aaaah!" Yo Yo screamed. The pain was almost too unbearable for Yo Yo to withstand. "All right man. Fuck, dog. It's in the bedroom, folks." Yo Yo's eyes started to water from the pain as John and Darryl pulled him from the couch and dragged him into the bedroom.

"Where's it at?" Kenny asked. Yo Yo pointed to a closet door adjacent to the bed. Darryl walked over to the walk-in closet and opened the door. He started to tear through the clothing and shoes in the big closet.

"Aye, yo, blood, ya'll ain't gotta tear up my shit. It's up on the top shelf in the Air Jordan boxes. Its thirty gees and a SKS in the back corner," Yo Yo said, trying to do damage control of his property.

Darryl grabbed the three shoeboxes off the top shelf. In each box was a stack of ten thousand in cash. Darryl kept searching the closet until he found the SKS behind a bloodred suit on a hanger in the back corner. Kenny went to work searching the red vanity dresser that set on the other side of the bedroom. He found two bags of chains, rings, watches, and bracelets.

"Aye, dog, some of them jew-wells are my bitch, shit!" Yo Yo protested.

John cocked back the hammer of the .357 he held on Yo Yo. "Shut the fuck up and tell us where the rest of the guns is at and the dope!" he shouted.

"Man, dog, fuck! I got a shotgun under the bed and a MAC-10 in the kitchen deep freezer and a half of key," Yo Yo said, shaking his head. Kenny smiled his ugly smile and flipped over the mattress to look for the shotgun instead. He found four rows of five thousand in cash, totaling twenty thousand.

"Somebody was holding out on us," he said.

"Naw, man, it ain't like that. I-I-I'm sorry, just don't hit me again," Yo Yo pleaded.

John swung the gun again, whacking Yo Yo in the face, splitting open his right cheek to the bone.

"Go check the freezer, Dee, while we clean all this shit up," Kenny said.

Darryl disappeared to search the kitchen for the gun and dope in the freezer. Both the gun and dope were where Yo Yo said they would be. When Darryl returned to the bedroom, Kenny was busy stuffing two duffel bags he had found in the closet with the money, bags of jewels, and the guns. Darryl squeezed the MAC-10 and half a key into the one of the full bags.

"That's everything, let's roll," Kenny said, grabbing the two duffle bags and leading the way out the house. John and Darryl picked Yo Yo up from the bedroom floor and started to lead him to the front door of the house.

Yo Yo stopped flat in his tracks and looked at John. "Aye, man, my fuckin' arm hurts. Can you flip the tape to the front or something? I gave ya'll everything. Why ya'll taken me from my tilt?" Yo Yo shook his head as he spoke.

"Retape him to the front," John said to Darryl. After he was retaped with his hands in front of him, he was led back to the taxi and put into the back seat of the car. "We're taking you back to your Cadillac, and you're free to go."

Darryl shut the cab door on Yo Yo and got behind the cab steering wheel. Kenny and John got into the Range Rover and drove off headed north. Darryl started up the cab, put it into gear, and drove off after the SUV and headed for Yo Yo's final resting place.

Yo Yo knew something was not right. These were dangerous men he was dealing with, and if they truly meant him no harm, they would have let him go on the spot at his home when he gave them all he had. No, these men intended to kill him, but Yo Yo had his mind made up. He would not go out peacefully.

Once they got off the freeway, Yo Yo took position, sliding down in the back seat, bringing his knees to his chest. He kicked forward with both feet with all his might, pushing forward the driver's seat. Darryl's body lurched forward from the kick. His forehead slammed into the steering wheel, dazing him. Yo Yo used both of his bound hands to open the car door and jump out while the cab coasted to a stop in the middle of the intersection. His body hit the street and started to roll. When he stopped moving, he got back to his feet and ran for his life. Darryl regained his composure just in time to see Yo Yo turning the corner on Lake Street. He bolted from the stalled cab in a sprint after Yo Yo. When he caught up to the bleeding gang member, Yo Yo was busy trying to cut the tape from his hands up against the stair railing of a vacant building. Darryl aimed a .38 snub nose Ruger he pulled out of his pants pocket. He pulled the trigger twice, sending two rounds into Yo Yo's back, clipping his spine and kidney. Yo Yo's body dropped like a sack of potatoes.

Darryl walked over Yo Yo's fallen body and pointed the gun down at him.

"I-I-I can't move, dog, I don't feel nothing," Yo Yo said as blood started to pool under him.

Kenny pulled the Range Rover to a stop at the curb next to the two men on the sidewalk. "Dee, no loose ends. Do that nigga right here and let's roll. Fuck the plan," Kenny said.

Darryl put the .38 against the temple of the bleeding man. "Man, come on, please no!" Yo Yo pleaded. Darryl pulled the trigger, releasing the last round from the cylinder into Yo Yo's skull. A fountain of blood and brain matter splattered all over his shoes, pants, legs, and the pavement.

"Damn, shit got all over me," Darryl said, checking the night streets for witnesses, but there were none.

"Fuck it, we gotta go. Get in, let's roll," John said. Darryl ran and jumped into the back seat of the Range Rover. Kenny put the truck in gear and drove the trio back to the freeway and headed back to the southwest side of town, where he paid for a small apartment he kept his mistress, Sunshine, in.

Kenny used Sunshine's place for all his business deals and meetings, such as the one they were about to have, because if he brought his crew home with a shitload of guns, drugs, and stolen jewels and money, his wife, Aida, would have a fit. Not Sunshine. She liked Kenny, and his business was his business, whatever that business was, as long as she benefited.

Sunshine was sound asleep when Kenny, John, and Darryl walked into the apartment. The three men went to work dividing the money, half a kilogram of cocaine, and the jewelry. Both Darryl and Kenny kept twenty-five thousand a piece; John took the twenty-seven because he wouldn't touch drugs. Kenny and Darryl split the powder cocaine in half. Kenny kept the SKS, and John took the MAC-10 while Darryl got the shotgun. Kenny disappeared into the bedroom and came back with a pair of shoes and pants for Darryl. He tossed him the keys to the Range Rover.

"Clean the truck from top to bottom. Make sure there's no blood in it, and burn your clothes and shoes. No loose ends, Darryl," Kenny advised. The three men celebrated a perfect score and agreed to meet back up at work later that day.

It was 2:00 a.m. when Darryl and John departed from Kenny and Sunshine's love nest. John left in his big white Ford F-250, and Darryl left in the Range Rover. Once they were gone, Kenny grabbed two chains, a figaro link and a snake chain, as well as a small diamond ring from the heist and crept into the bedroom. He stripped down to his boxers and slid into the bed next to his sleeping mistress. He reached over her and put the jewelry next to the bed onto the bedside table. Sunshine didn't budge. She continued to sleep. Kenny just laid in bed and watched her sleep, taking in her beauty. *She is even more beautiful in her slumber,* Kenny thought. He wondered if he should just leave Aida and marry Sunshine since he thought he loved his mistress more. They were the last thoughts he entertained before he lost consciousness and fell asleep. Kenny's eyes came open a few hours later with Sunshine before him, bouncing up and down on the bed like a schoolgirl, wearing both chains around her neck. Kenny leaned back on his elbows, looking at Sunshine as though he were seeing her for the first time—his Afro-Latin princess, with her creamy tan skin and flawless beauty. He loved her dark eyes and long eye lashes. Her perfectly positioned nose and precisely arched eyebrows. Most of all, he loved her radiant smile that truly made the sun shine.

"Thank you, Daddy," she said, climbing off the bed and going over to a full-length mirror to look over herself in her new jewelry. Kenny watched her move in front of the mirror. She put her hand on her long, slender neck, running her fingers across the gold chains; she stood seductively in front of the mirror and tossed her waist-long hair over her left shoulder. Kenny noticed her small pear-shaped breast and nipples protruding through the flower nightgown she wore. The fabric hung loosely to the curves of her tight petite body, the gown stopping short mid-thigh, exposing her long legs and small bare feet. "I love them, Kenny, where they come from?" she asked, crawling back into the bed, letting her hair fall back over her shoulder.

"I got them last night," he said, watching her move toward him on her hands and knees. She positioned herself on top of him, straddling his mid-lower half; she brought herself down until they were face-to-face.

"I love you," she said, closing her eyes, kissing Kenny in the lips. Kenny pulled back, disengaging from the lip-lock. She opened her eyes, searching his face for signs of his withdrawal, but there was none.

"Did you get the ring?" he asked. Sunshine looked confused. She had been so absorbed with the chains she overlooked the ring on the nightstand by the bed. "It's by the phone on the nightstand," he directed.

She stayed in her position on top of Kenny as she leaned over and pulled the ring from the nightstand, looking it over before she put it on her marriage finger. Sunshine smiled, admiring the big diamond protruding from the center of the gold band wrapped around her finger. "Are we getting married now? Does this mean you're leaving her?" she asked.

Kenny weighed his options. His wife, Aida, was his rock; she loved him without condition. At twenty-eight, she wasn't a twenty-four-year-old free spirit like Sunshine was, but Kenny knew she would be with him come hell or high water when Sunshine wouldn't. Knowing what he knew, he still felt torn between the two women. "Soon, mami," he said.

"No, I'm tired of waiting, Kenny. I'm tired of living in that bitch Aida's shadow!" Sunshine screamed, pulling the ring from her finger, throwing a child's tantrum and chucking the ring across the room.

"What the fuck are you doing?" Kenny said.

"You love my sorry as cousin more than you love me! I hate her, and I hate you!" she screamed in Kenny's face.

Sunshine tried to jump out of the bed, but he grabbed her by both shoulders. "What's wrong with you? I told you I was going to be with you, didn't I? This shit takes some time, Sunshine. I don't want to hurt you or Aida. I love you. I am not in love with her, but I don't want to hurt her, so let me do this. We're going to be together, do you understand?" he reasoned.

Sunshine nodded with tears in her eyes. She leaned forward and started kissing him again. Kenny stuck his hand underneath her nightgown, feeling the moisture between her legs. Sunshine was becoming excited. Kenny realized it was Sunshine's sexual drive that kept him from making the righteous decision, which was to end his deceptive affair with his wife's cousin. Sunshine returned to her straddling position, slowly lowering herself onto Kenny. She started a slow up-and-down motion, increasing her speed until she reached her climax. Kenny followed shortly after and fell back into an early-morning slumber.

ANOTHER DAY AT
THE OFFICE

Sunshine was in the kitchen cooking bacon and eggs when Kenny got out of the shower. He put on the fresh clothes he laid out on the bed fresh out of the cleaners. He put on a pair of blue Rocawear jeans and blue nylon Nike Cortez with a white check. He put on a white tank top, followed by a bulletproof vest; then he covered the vest with a thick, white Pro Club T-shirt and white Los Angeles Dodgers jersey with blue trim. Kenny took the red rubber bands off the tips of his braids and changed them out for blue rubber bands then put on the blue pinstriped white LA Dodgers hate. He grabbed the 9 mm he kept in the closet with the military holster cup he kept it in. He ran the harness inside of his jersey and clipped the holster under his left arm. He walked over to the dresser and picked up a clear tube of powder cocaine. Once he was dressed, he walked into the living room of the apartment and sorted five thousand out of the twenty-five he had gotten off the Yo heist, then he went into the kitchen where Sunshine was preparing his plate. He put five grand on the countertop.

"Take care of shit around here or whatever you do," Kenny said, pulling a black plastic bag from a trash-bag roller he put over the trash can, then he walked out of the kitchen, took the remainder of the eight ounces of cocaine, and stuffed them into the plastic bag.

Sunshine sat a plate of bacon and eggs down in front of Kenny; she took a seat across from him and watched him eat. When he finished eating, Kenny pulled the cocaine tube from his pocket, opened the vial, and poured a healthy amount between his index finger and thumb. He put his right hand up to his nose and inhaled the white powder until it was all gone. Kenny pushed away from the kitchen table and picked up his cell phone from off the coffee table in the living room. He picked up the pager next to the phone and punched in the seven numbers to his boy Cyco from the Sunset Neighborhood Crip set. "Aye, cuzz, what's up? It's K-Loc." Kenny said.

"What's crackin', my nigga?" Cyco said.

"I got eight zones for you, my nigga, soft sale," Kenny proposed.

"What they goin' foe?" Cyco asked.

"Give me six for all of them," Kenny bargained.

"Aight, cuzz, come by the hood spot. My boy BadLuck will bring you to the house, and I'll have the scratch, cuzz," Cyco said.

"All right, loc out," Kenny said, closing his cell phone and cancelling the call. The powder seemed to shoot straight to his brain as Kenny walked out of the apartment to his car with the bag of powder cocaine. He pulled the keys out of his pocket and pushed the car's disarm button, taking the alarm's sensor off his blue 2007 Dodge Charger on twenty-inch chrome Larenzo rims. Kenny got into his car, buckled his safety belt, and sped off into the streets of Sunset with the four subwoofers blasting C-Bo's antipolice anthem "Deadly Game" from his *Till My Casket Drops* album.

Kenny had a lot to do, and he planned to work all night, so he told Sunshine not to wait up for him. Kenny slammed the gas pedal down on the Charger's firewall, burning rubber and sending the car flying top speed southwest toward the Sunset city ghetto to the Crip neighborhood.

It was 12:00 p.m. when Kenny reached the neighborhood of the Sunset Neighborhood Crips. Kenny slowed his speed as he navigated through the ragged streets filled with potholes and broken glass. This seemed to be a difficult task since he was high on cocaine; still, he tried his best to protect the Parelli tires that wrapped the Larenzo rims. Kenny studied the wall's graffiti as he sped by; they were scribbled with SS NHC Gang and BS KILLA for the Blood Side Gang, whom they were involved in a vicious turf war with. He blasted his music at max volume as he drove top speed once he got out of the fractured streets.

As he passed an alley, he caught a glimpse of what he believed to be an old lady being mugged. He slammed on the brakes, skidding to a stop; he put the car in reverse and backed up, blocking the alley off. There was a white junky struggling with an elderly black woman for her purse. Kenny put the car in park, opened the car door, got out, flung himself across the car hood, and landed next to the struggling pair, who were both oblivious of his arrival because of their struggle. Kenny pulled the pistol from his shoulder holster and struck the white man hard across the back of the head with the butt of the gun. The mugger fell to the ground on his side and tried to cover himself from further assault. Kenny jumped down on top of the would-be thief and continued to strike him in the face and arms, swelling up his flesh and ripping his skin open. Kenny was losing his control trying to kill the white man.

The older woman grabbed him, pulling him off the broken white man, saving him from plunging off the deep end into the dark side. Kenny stood back up, regaining his composure. He brushed the dirt off his jersey and put his gun back in the holster.

"Thank you, sir," the old woman said. Kenny smiled, brushing the dirt off his pants. He felt prideful. He knew any other time he would just keep driving, but that didn't fit his plan today. "It is good to know there are still some good, courageous young black men in the world today," she said.

Kenny got back into his car and threw his left fist out of the window as he drove off, signaling black power. Kenny swerved off from the alley, leaving the man beaten half to death. He didn't feel an ounce of pity for the guy. He was doing what he normally did. Kenny did what he did, but why was he so vicious? He wondered that maybe it was the coke.

Kenny arrived on L Avenue at 1:30 p.m. There was about six or seven men hanging in front of Cyco's dope spot. Most of them wore blue clothing, but Kenny could see they all wore gun bulges in the front of their waistbands under their shirts. There were several expensive cars parked on the grass in the driveway and on the curb. Kenny saw two Chevy Suburban's, three lowriders, a Chevy Avalanche, and a Lexus. All with candy-paint jobs, chrome rims, and gold Daytons. There was nowhere for Kenny to park, so he blew the horn three times in the middle of the street. One of the men walked away from the crowd and came over to the Charger. Kenny recognized the man as BadLuck as he opened the door and slid into the passenger seat of his car and closed the door. Kenny turned the music down in the car to a low rumble in the trunk.

"What's up, K-Loc?" BadLuck said, shaking Kenny's hand.

"Nothin', cuzz, tryna handle this bizz," he answered.

"Yeah, fa'sho. Push it up the avenue, cuzz," BadLuck advised. Kenny slammed his foot down, burning rubber in front of the gang house three blocks. "Stop right here, loc," BadLuck said. Kenny pulled to a stop in front of a big white house with a blue '64 Chevy Impala in the driveway. There was a Mercedes Bens S-Class parked behind the lowrider. "Hit the horn, cuzz," BadLuck said. Kenny pushed down on the car horn twice, and the two men waited until the front door of the house opened and a large light-skinned man with a long black ponytail stepped out with a small black bag. He wore a thin tan linen suit, a long chain with a diamond-encrusted pendent, a platinum watch, and two large diamond earrings. He walked to the car and got into the back seat of the Charger.

"What's up, K-Loc?" he said, putting the small bag on the seat next to him.

"What's up Cyco, cuzz," Kenny said in greeting.

"Let's do it movin' around the block a few times," Cyco said, pulling the five grand out of his small bag. Kenny put the car in motion, sending it around the corner as they spoke. "Aye you heard about the nigga Yo Yo gettin' lamped?" Cyco asked.

"Yeah, cuzz, I saw that shit on the news. Niggas smoked that nigga and two moe of them fools. Ya'll did that?" Kenny asked the SS NHC kingpin.

Cyco laughed. "Naw, I thought that was ya'll," he said, referring to the One Six Sunset Crip set he believed Kenny to be from. The OSSSC and SS NHC gangs were allies and shared the Blood Side Gang as enemies.

"You know how that shit be, loc. That probably was the Lil homies or something caught them bitch-ass niggas slippin'. Here go the zips," Kenny said, handing the black plastic bag of cocaine ounces over his shoulder to Cyco.

"Yeah, that's what's up, cuzz," he said, looking into the bag at the powder.

Kenny pulled the car to a stop in front of Cyco's residence and handed Kenny the five grand in the bag, and then another thought he pulled from his own pocket. "What else is up, Cyco? What's crackin' out here on these streets?" Kenny asked, counting the money, he had been handed.

"Shit, we ain't been able to focus on bussin' on the BS niggas 'cause we keep getting' into it with these fuckin' Mexicans from the Montoya Cartel. The homies went through and popped on them niggas," Cyco said, confusing Kenny.

"Why what's up with the Montoya Cartel?" he asked, intrigued.

"Them muthafuckas is moving dope straight across the Mexican border, flooding the south side of Sunset, which is fuckin' off our economy, cuzz. I'm going to set up a meeting to see if we can cut some kind of deal on some birds. If not, they gotta go, loc," Cyco said sternly.

Kenny knew the Montoya Cartel well, and to him, it sounded like Cyco was about to wage a turf war that the SS NHCs could not win. The Montoya Cartel were not the average pushovers like Yo Yo and the BS Gang; the Montoyas had real firepower.

"K-Loc, is One Sixe down if we gotta push these fools outta Sunset?" Cyco asked.

"Yeah, loc, we're down. I'll holla at the homies don't trip," he said. Cyco got out of the car, and Kenny drove back down the avenue to drop BadLuck back off at the gang house, then he pushed the car across town. He knew he still had to deal with some drama at work. He felt exhausted and wished he didn't have to go into the office. He held the steering wheel with his left hand and fished the tube of coke out of his pocket with his right hand. He pulled the cap off with his teeth as he swerved the Charger on the freeway through the rush-hour traffic. He poured the powder onto a piece of paper and held it to his nose; he made sure he maintained his speed as he inhaled the cocaine—a technique he has perfected over the years.

Kenny arrived at his job at 3:16 p.m., sixteen minutes late. He looked himself over in the rearview mirror and saw trails of white powder in his nostrils. He opened up the glove box and pulled out a few fast-food restaurant napkins and blew his nose. Then he noticed dried blood flakes speckled on his jersey, which he had not seen before. "Damn it," he said, getting out of his car and walking to his trunk. He took off the jersey and changed it out for a blue checkered Ralph Lauren button-down polo shirt he kept in the trunk for times like these. He left the shirt open so that he could have access to his shoulder holster. He took one last look at himself in the car's side-view mirror. He was clean and neat.

Kenny walked into his office and went straight to his desk; he plopped down in his swivel chair and took a load off. He put his feet up on the desk and watched his coworkers move about around him. He saw Nicole Brown, a small Indian and black–mix woman. She stood five foot four and was 130 pounds. She had an hourglass figure with large full breast, a flat stomach, wide hips, and a fat ass. She always had a look on her face that read, "I know I'm the shit, clown." She sat on Tamino Sanches's desk, laughing.

Kenny liked Tamino, a fat slob of a man of Mexican descent, who was always telling jokes. Kenny focused his attention on Jenny Hall, a tall, skinny, blond white woman with big fake breasts spilling out of a hooker's outfit. She leaned over Sam Garboski's desk, putting her cleavage in his face. Kenny hated Sam, but he could deal with Jenny because she was just what she portrayed to be: a whore. Sam was a racist who was trying to no doubt break himself to pay her for sex when Kenny usually got it for free from her.

He looked off to his left, observing Danny Zamora shuffling through files at his desk. Danny was a good kid but took his job a little too serious. Maybe if he worried a little less about his job, his wife wouldn't be getting banged by his best friend, Ricky Gomez. Everybody at the office knew Ricky was sticking it to Danny's wife, and that included Danny. Danny was a skinny Mexican with a thick, frizzy afro; Ricky was his complete opposite. He was taller and built like Arnold Schwarzenegger with a bald head and a handlebar mustache.

"Kenny! Kenny!" John called from the back of the office. "Come on back!"

Kenny got up from his desk and walked to the backroom where John was huddled at Darryl's desk with Darryl and their boss, Steven Dooner. The three men were looking over the Sunset homicide detective's murder book, laughing. Kenny looked down at the book to see several photos of Yo Yo's bullet lobotomized corpse on the sidewalk.

"I did my best to make this murder look gang-related," Darryl said.

"What about the stolen cab?" Kenny asked skeptically.

"I cleaned it down. There's no prints on it. Don't trip," Darryl said.

"Who's on the case with you?" Kenny asked.

"Tamino," Darryl answered, easing Kenny's nerves. He knew Tamino was lazy and not going to do too much work on any case.

The small gathering was broken up as Thomas O'Brien, the head chief of the Sunset Police Department, stepped out of his office and stared down the homicide detectives. "Detectives Johnson, Zamora, Lake, Brown, McBeth, and Hall, in my office now!" the chief screamed.

INTERNAL AFFAIRS

Kenny walked into the chief's office after the homicide division sergeant. Steven Dooner, Nicole, Darryl, John, Danny, and Jenny followed behind him. Kenny sat in a small straight-back chair. Everybody else either took a seat or stood. Once everyone was situated, the chief, an overly fat man of Irish descent, took the floor to speak.

"First and foremost, we have the fuckin' IA breathing down our fucking neck. They're wondering like I've been wondering how some are living so well off basic detective salaries. You know who you are," he said, shooting a look at Kenny, who met his glare head-on, making the chief turn red in the face. "I want full reports on my desk within the hour of all undercover investigations. Do not leave out any details. It can cost you your gun and your badge. Do you all understand?" he continued his speech. The group all acknowledged their understanding to the chief and started to file out to write their reports. The sergeant stayed behind to try to do damage control with the chief.

Kenny was not happy with the chief's briefing. The Internal Affairs was trouble—trouble he did not need. Kenny scribbled down a completely false report about his investigations into the Sunset

Neighborhood Crips. There was no way Kenny wanted to give his boss or the IA leads that would link his under-the-table currency flow to him bank rolling the SS NHC Gang house. When Kenny finished, he turned his report into the chief himself.

"Good, I wanted to see your file first to see what one of Sunset's highest-paid detectives has really been up to," the chief said, opening the folder Kenny had handed him. Kenny left the chief's office without responding. He went back to his desk and tried to focus. He was worried sick about the IA coming to investigate the homicide division. He also wondered why Garboski, Sanches, and Gomez weren't called into the meeting. Were they telling what little they may have known or seen?

Kenny picked up his desk phone and hit the speed dial to the house he lived in with his wife. The phone rang for a spell, then it was answered. "Hello." Her voice sounded like music to Kenny's ears.

"What's up, baby?" he said.

"Kenny, how are you? Are you all right? I called the office last night, and they said you had not been in, called, or checked in. Where were you? I was worried sick," she started, worry and concern in her voice.

"Calm down, Lil Mama. I was deep undercover, and I couldn't call, but I'm all right. I've missed you," he said. The line went silent for a moment, then he heard soft whimpering sounds over the phone. *Damn, not this shit not now,* he said to himself. Dealing with an emotional Aida was the last thing he wanted to do, but he knew he would have to. "What's the matter, Aida?" he asked.

"I've missed you too, Kenny. You're never home, I hardly see you. There is something I have to tell you," she said, debating whether she wanted to drop the H-bomb she had in store.

"What, Aida?" He asked.

"Kenny, are you cheating on me? Is there someone else?" she asked.

"What are you crazy? Where would you get some shit like that?" He imitated anger and concern; after all, it was his job to fake for the best results as an undercover homicide detective.

"I don't know, Kenny. It just feels like your drifting away and I'm losing you." She sobbed.

"Aida, I'll be home tonight, and we'll talk then, not like this over the phone, all right? I would never leave you or cheat on you. You gotta believe that, Aida," he lied.

"I'll talk to you when you come home then, Kenny," she said, still in tears.

Good, Kenny thought. Now he could get to the question he called to ask. "Aida, has any cops been by the house in suits to talk to you?" he asked.

"No, why? Were they supposed to?" she asked.

"No, don't worry, but if you see anyone, don't tell them anything, Aida, nothing. Tell them you don't know nothing and for them to contact me, all right?" he asked her.

"All right, Kenny. Are you in some kind of trouble?" she asked, concerned.

"No, I'm fine. I gotta go, baby, I love you," he said, hanging up the phone.

Kenny walked over to John's desk and sat on the edge. "Fucking bitch," he said, closing the folder. He had just filled some facts and some lies about the undercover job he was working with Danny Zamora on some Jewish mafia armed robberies. "I just finished my report. I hope the bastard is happy," he said.

Darryl joined them at John's desk. "I need a suspect for the Yo Yo Bobby Jenkins murder, preferably a Sunset Crip. Got anybody in mind?" he asked Kenny.

Kenny thought for a while, then it hit him. "I got a guy named BadLuck. He is perfect for the job," he said.

"Cool," Darryl said.

"Aye, Johnny, what do we do about the IA? They are going to be on us soon," Kenny said.

John leaned back in his chair and put his feet up onto his desk, balancing the chair on two legs. "We do what we've been doing, getting paid on and off the job. Fuck the IA, they ain't got shit on us," he said smugly.

Kenny was burning with rage. Will and self-control were the only things that kept him from kicking the greedy Jewish man out of his chair. "Johnny, have you forgotten about Gorboski?" Kenny asked, forcing John to think back a year ago when Kenny, Darryl, Sam, and himself were working a case on the Mexican Locos, a Sunset Latino gang. One of the gang members recognized John from a prior arrest when John was a beat cop; once he was made, John did not intend to let the man get away. They chased him down to an abandoned warehouse. Darryl tackled the man to the ground while John walked over him and pumped two rounds into the man's skull right in front of Sam Garboski, saving the mission but leaving the team in a situation. In a panic, Kenny and John lured another of the ML gang to the warehouse. John handed him the same gun he had shot and killed the first man with and made him fire the weapon at some targets he had erected out of old crates and bottles. Then he was given the pistol and told he could leave. Everybody swore not to speak a word about the murder, and weeks later, Kenny and Darryl arrested the Mexican Loco gang member, who still had the murder weapon with his fingerprints on it and had him tried and convicted. Things were well until Sam and Kenny started to bump heads. First, they clashed over Sam calling a black drug dealer a nigger and beating him half to death with a side handle baton. The same day, Kenny stormed into the office, got the same side handle baton from evidence, and walked over to Garboski's desk while Sam was filling out his paperwork from his incident. Kenny started to beat the detective to a bloody pulp, almost losing his cool. What was worse was Sam threatened to call the IA if Kenny ever touched him again. Now with the IA knocking on the department's front door, there was no telling what Sam Garboski was capable of.

"Yeah, you're right. Garboski has got to go," John said, realizing Kenny raised a solid issue.

The Internal Affairs had not even arrived yet, and they were scrambling like mad men. "So who's going to do it?" Kenny asked.

John looked to Darryl, who looked down at the floor. Kenny didn't like what he was seeing. "Look, Kenny, man, we're already in too deep. We can't just whack a UC right up under the IA's noses," Darryl said. Kenny could sense his fear and that pissed him off.

"John, it's me and you. You in?" he asked.

"Yeah, I'm in," the short Jewish man said.

"Good. Darryl, you're out. I'll do this shit myself," Kenny said, putting on a pair of black isotoners he picked up off John's desk. "We'll need that MAC-10 we got from Yo Yo and the Desert Eagle. Darryl, the Desert Eagle is in the truck glove compartment. Bring it back here and drop the truck off at Sunshine's. John, help him out and get that Mac."

"What are you going to do?" John asked.

"I'm going to pick us out a car. Don't forget to get me that gun, John," Kenny said and walked out the office, heading toward the impounded vehicle parking lot. Kenny walked down the rows of stolen and seized cars from numerous drug bust and other crimes. He couldn't make up his mind on the car he wanted off the top, so he cruised the lanes. He stopped in front of a big yellow Toyota Titan 4×4 truck. Kenny looked the big truck over as a whole, but chose against it. It was too big for what he had planned.

He kept walking down the rows, then stopped again in front of a two-tone brown-and-white 1986 Buick Regal on thirteen-inch chrome Roadsters. He continued the search; the Regal would cause too much attention to be drawn to his mission, and he needed stealth. What he needed was plain, so his eyes lit up when he spotted a factory-green painted 1995 Chevy Impala Super Sport with stock Five Star rims and mirror-tinted windows. Kenny walked over to the checkout. The officer on duty had his face buried in a Spider-Man comic book while Kenny took the sign-out book and signed in Sergeant Steven Dooner's name for the Impala; once he was signed in, Kenny waited impatiently while the kid continued to view the comic.

"Ha ha, ole', Spidey." He chuckled. Kenny slammed his hand down on the checkout cage's counter.

"Oh, excuse me, sir," the young officer said, putting down the comic book. "What number will that be?"

"Number 226," Kenny said.

The attendant turned around to the key wall and searched for number 226. "Here we go," he said, turning around and handling the key to Kenny.

Kenny left the lot in the Impala and parked it around the corner from the police department. Around the back of the station was a shady back street. He knew the car wouldn't be seen until it was needed. When Kenny returned to his desk in the station, John and Darryl had already left to pick up the MAC-10 and the Desert Eagle and drop his truck off. He put his head down on his desk and fell asleep. Kenny was sleep for over an hour. He was woken up by the crackling sounds of Sam Garboski's laughter. Kenny shot him a look of irritation. Sam ignored his gaze and continued his acts of court jester, entertaining Tamino, Jenny, and Danny, who laughed uncontrollably. Darryl and John walked back into the office and took the two chairs in front of his desk.

"Aye, dog, I would have done it. I just got a lot of shit on my mind, like the IA and all that other shit," Darryl said. He knew he had pissed

Kenny off earlier, and he was trying to get back in his good graces. He handed Kenny the Desert Eagle.

"It ain't nothing, Dee, I'll take care of it," Kenny said, taking the Desert Eagle and putting it into an empty plastic evidence bag. He pulled out his bottom desk drawer, opened his hollow stash box behind the drawer, and put the bag inside with a few ecstasy pills and cocaine.

"Lake, Johnson, my office now!" Sergeant Dooner shouted.

"Damn, man, what the hell now?" Kenny said as both men got up and headed for the sergeant's office. They sat in the two vacant chairs before his desk. Steven Dooner was a strictly business, older, overweight black man with a gray Afro. The forty-six-year old sat behind his desk in his swivel chair like a king on his throne and tossed two folders across the desk at Kenny and Darryl. Both men looked inside the two folders, which were files detailing the daily functions and operations of the Montoya Cartel. There were two black-and-white mug shots in front of them on the sergeant's desk.

"Gentlemen, the photos on the desk are mug shots of Umberto and Rodamez Montoya, the kingpins of the Montoya Cartel. Are you familiar with them?" the sergeant asked. Kenny nodded while Darryl shook his head no. "What do you know, Lake?" the sergeant asked.

"My NHC connect was telling me the Montoyas are flooding the market, and they plan on having a sit-down before the shit really hit the fan."

"So does your connect have an in?" Darryl asked Kenny.

"No, they're just trying to keep them from regulating the drug trade," he said.

The sergeant sat down at his desk, smiling. "That all sounds good. Here is the thing that red piece of shit O'Brien is breathing down my neck. The IA is breathing down his neck, so, Kenny, we'll need to toss the SS NHCs to O'Brien. That way the IA can see us at work. Then you and Danny can infiltrate the Montoya Cartel, all the while gathering discreetly what riches we can. I'll need a full-scale report for the raid on the SS NHCs by the week's end," he said.

Kenny nodded in agreement, rising from the chair with the Montoya file in hand. Darryl followed behind him. Writing another report was the last thing Kenny wanted to do. He would rather focus on killing Garboski.

Darryl went back to his own desk to work on his report for O'Brien. Kenny went to work, pausing briefly to answer a phone call from Sunshine.

"Yeah," Kenny said into the cell phone, checking his watch; it was almost 7:30 p.m.

"Are you coming over tonight? I'm sorry about this morning, and I want to make it up to you," she said.

Kenny envisioned Sunshine having things her way and making up to him. He wished he didn't have to work or see Aida 'cause he would be back at her apartment with bells on. "I can't, baby, I gotta work all night. You know how I get caught up sometimes," he said. Actually, she didn't; she had no idea where Kenny worked. She thought he was a dealer, but that didn't bother her.

"You're still not mad at me, Kenny, are you? I'm sorry for real," she said.

Kenny laughed. "Naw, I ain't mad. I just can't make it. Believe me, if I could, I would," he said.

"Darryl dropped off yo truck. If you can, please come over," she said.

"I'll try. All right, I gotta go," he said.

"Kenny, wait!" she shouted. "I love you."

"Ditto," he said, closing the phone.

SOMEBODY'S GOT TO DIE

Kenny finished filling out the report and tactical strategy for his raid on the Sunset Neighborhood Crips just as John came back out of O'Brien's office and sat down at his desk. "I got the MAC-10 in my truck. When you want to put this bitch down?" he asked.

"We'll hit that fool tonight after he gets off work. I gotta turn this report in. Let's roll," he said, rising from his desk with the report in his hand. John walked with him into the sergeant's office. Kenny tossed the folder on the sergeant's desk. "It's all there, Sarge," Kenny said.

"All right, I'll prepare the mission, and I'll call you both tomorrow," Steven said, reaching for the folder. The phone on his desk started to ring. The sergeant held up a hand to both the men, waving them off.

"We're off the clock, Sarge," Kenny said as he and John walked out of the office. Kenny closed the door behind them as Steven picked up the phone.

"What was that all about?" John asked, stopping at his desk to cut off his desk lamp.

"It was the blueprints for a raid on the NHCs," Kenny said, cutting off the light at his desk as well.

"Hopefully that'll buy us some time with O'Brien and the IA. You want to go get something to eat until this jackass gets off?" John asked.

"Yeah, sure, why not? I'm starving," Kenny said.

As the two detectives walked out of the station, they passed two people they had never seen before. Kenny eyed the pair skeptically as they passed, studying both himself and John. Kenny took in their fancy business suits, briefcases, and Colgate smiles and recognized them for who they were. They were the Internal Affairs.

"Damn, they're here," Kenny mumbled under his breath to John. They studied the odd pair briefly. There was a white yet tan woman who stood six one. Her long, black hair was parted on one side and wrapped behind her head in a conservative tight bun. She had professionally arched eyebrows with large dark-blue eyes; she had high cheekbones and a thin nose, which gave her face an elegant appearance. She had big, full lips and a beautiful smile. The woman's body was amazing. She had extremely large breasts, the size of cantaloupes, a firm butt, and long legs. She wore a tight gray pantsuit that clung to her shape and curvaceous body. Kenny wondered if she worked out in her spare time.

The man was another story. He was of Asian descent with a long, black ponytail and a full beard. He was five eight, 120 five pounds. He was all around smaller than the female agent was. It made them look odd, but the Asian man was also neat and clean in his black suit and tie. The two agents stopped beside the two detectives.

"Hi, I'm Internal Affairs agent Audra Solis, and this is Agent Peter Chan," she said, extending her soft hand to first Kenny then John. Kenny noticed quickly that she spoke her introduction with a southern accent, which made him wonder where this white woman with the country bumpkin accent got a name like Solis.

"I'm detective Kenny Lake, and this is detec—"

"And you must be John McBeth," Audra said, finishing the introduction. Kenny knew his face revealed his horror that the IA knew exactly who he and John were.

"You're not from around here, are you?" he asked, trying to cover with small talk.

"No, I'm not, I'm from Georgia," she said, blushing. She checked her watch; it was 9:30 p.m. "It's getting late, Detective Lake. I have to go. I hope to see you soon," she said, smiling and walking off.

Kenny got a chill as the two agents walked away. He got into his Charger and drove around the corner of the police station where he had the Impala SS parked out of view. John followed behind him in his Ford F-250 truck. Once Kenny parked his car, he snorted a line of cocaine and got into the truck with John. They went to eat at a small café. After they ate, John drove them back to the Impala. Kenny got the MAC-10 from underneath the front seat of John's truck. They loaded into the Impala and headed to the police station parking lot.

Kenny sat in the passenger seat of the green Chevy Impala; John sat in the driver's seat behind the wheel. It was 10:45 p.m. when Sam Garboski walked out of the station with a briefcase. He got into his blue factory-painted 1996 Chevy Lumina; he settled in, put the car key into the ignition, and started the car. He turned up the volume of his favorite country song on his stock radio and turned his car onto Avenger Avenue, coming out of the police station parking lot.

"Ah, what a day," he said, nodding his head to the tune of his music as he let his mind wonder to thoughts of his son, Sam Junior, who was an up-and-coming football player with dreams of going pro. Then he thought about Jenny Hall's breast and ass and realized how much he hated his wife, Murphy. Sam made a quick left on Authers Lane, then a quick right into a small alley where he always picked up hookers. Sam always entrapped streetwalkers by soliciting them for cheap sex, then flashing his badge. Most of the girls were more than willing to trade sexual favors for a get-out-of-jail-free pass. He checked his rearview mirror and saw the '96 Chevy Impala in the alley in the distance. He may have paid the car more attention had it not been for the black woman walking down the alley in a small white mini skirt, tight tank top, and small purse. Liking what he saw, he pulled to a stop next to the young street pro.

"You workin', girl?" he asked.

"Yeah, Daddy, what you talkin'?" she said, stepping to the passenger side of the detective's car.

John turned off the Impala's lights as he saw Sam pull over for the prostitute, then he drove slowly toward the Lumina.

"So how much you charge for everything, sweetness?" Sam asked. Sam's words fell on deaf ears because the girl's attention had shifted to the approaching car with tinted windows. "Aye, girl, what's the matter? Cat got your tongue?" he said, first studying the girl then looking back over his shoulder at what had her attention. He saw a green Impala cruising down the alley toward them. Sam did not like what he saw, so he went for the .38 special he kept in the glove box of his car. He fumbled with the gun, looking over his shoulder as the passenger's tinted window rolled down, and he saw Kenny's face and an MAC-10. Kenny saw Sam reaching for what he believed to be a gun in the glove box; Sam's seatbelt was keeping him from getting full access into the box. When John pulled the Impala to a stop next to the Chevy Lumina, Kenny rolled down the window and stuck the MAC-10 out almost into Sam's car. Sam stared down the barrel of the submachine gun as Kenny squeezed the trigger. The MAC-10 jerked in his hand spitting hot lead into the detective's head and neck. The ten hollow tips ate the flesh from his face, mutilating the dying man's face. Sam's body went limp and tried to slump to the right, but the seatbelt straining against his overweight frame kept him erect.

Kenny sprayed off another twelve rounds through the left side of Sam's ribs, stomach, and his left arm. John grabbed Kenny's left shoulder to stop him from shooting. When he stopped squeezing off rounds, Kenny could hear the prostitute screaming her head off. He re-aimed the MAC-10 on the screaming woman and sprayed her down with six rounds from the thirty-round MAC-10 magazine. John slammed his foot down on the Impala gas pedal, sending the big V8-motored vehicle shooting down the alley to Avenger Avenue, and drove back around the corner from the police department. Both men got out of the Impala and headed to their vehicles.

"There is such a thing as overkill, Kenny. You didn't have to lamp the girl," John said, climbing into his truck with the MAC-10. He started up the F-250 and drove off, leaving Kenny in the street getting into his car. Kenny stared after John's truck, turning the corner.

"Fuck John and his kids," he said, starting up his Charger. He shifted into gear and sped off to the freeway. Once Kenny got on the freeway, he performed his snorting-while-rolling ritual, flying eastbound toward the home he shared with his wife, Aida. Under the influence of the powder cocaine, Kenny turned a two-hour drive into an hour flat. Kenny pulled to a stop in front of his two-story house on Sunset Hills. Aida's gray 2007 Mercedes SL Coupe was parked in the driveway behind Kenny's midnight-blue 2006 Ford Mustang GT.

Kenny walked across the large front lawn and fished his keys out of his front right pocket, stuck them in the lock, and unlocked his illegally financed palace. Kenny's house was furnished with floor-to-ceiling wall mirrors, blue leather couches with white trim, white carpet, a big stainless steel kitchen, a gym room, living room, dining room, a swimming pool, three bathrooms, six bedrooms, big flat screen TVs, DVD players, and glass chandeliers. Aida had done all the house decorating, and most of the stuff was overrated to Kenny, but he still let her do her thing. There was also a spa and a two-car garage in the big backyard. Kenny slipped into the main shower in his bedroom bathroom.

It was 11:30 p.m. When Kenny stepped out of the shower, he checked himself over before drying off because Aida knew nothing about his drug abuse. After he made sure he was clean, he made his way into the bedroom where he saw his wife lying on their bed, naked. It had been days since Kenny had seen his wife. He felt bad for neglecting his wife, but sometimes he gets so wrapped up in Sunshine he would lose his way. Seeing her now, he did not know how he could.

Aida was a dime. She came from a black, Cuban, and Indian background, which gave her an almost orange complexion. Her long, black hair with brown highlights hung down past her shoulders, falling to her mid-lower back. She had a square hairline, which gave her a unique look, enhancing her beauty. Aida's eyebrows were thick at the front but thinned as they ended and looked as though they were locked in an adorable questioning look. She had the hugest brown eyes, which seemed to make her look pouty. Her nose was perfect, and she had a small overbite because her top lip was a little bit bigger than her lower lip. There were smile lines around her mouth where age had touched her face, but she was still angelic to Kenny. Her body was the mold God used to design the thickest woman to ever walk the earth that was not fat, and then he broke the mold. Her measurements were 34-21-36, and she was still a gem at twenty-eight.

Kenny smiled looking at her. Her stomach was still flat, her breast were still perky, and her butt was still firm. Kenny slid onto the bed and crawled in between her thighs. He looked into her eyes, realizing he missed her. He started to kiss and lick her body from head to toe; he concentrated on her breast then her navel and between her thighs. Aida was pleased by her husband's experienced tongue strokes until her passion and pleasure spilled over. Kenny let his hands travel up and down his wife's smooth and shaved center. He pulled her legs apart, exposing her to him like a peeled peach. He dove in deep until he became one with his wife. She let out little moans, which turned into howls as she reached an earth-moving second climax. When Kenny was finished, he rolled over to relax.

"Kenny that was mind-blowing," she said, climbing on top of him.

"It was, huh?" he said, rubbing her butt.

"I'm glad I waited up for you." She waited up for him for more than sex, and when she saw him smiling and at peace, she figured it was no better time to tell him.

"Kenny, I'm pregnant," she said, kissing his chest and stomach.

"What?" Kenny half asked, half screamed.

Aida detected disappointment in Kenny. "I said I'm pregnant. You're going to be a father. Are you mad?" she asked.

"Mad? Mad for what? This is great news," he lied.

"Really, Kenny?" she asked, filled with excitement.

"Of course it is. Come here," he said, pulling her into an embrace. Kenny could not get any sleep after Aida dropped her bomb on him. He was not ready to become a father. He waited until Aida went to sleep, took a quick shower, and drove across town to Sunshine's apartment. He woke up again after spending the majority of the morning bangin' out Sunshine's brains. The sun had already rose, and he was exhausted, but he knew he had to get back across town. Being with Sunshine though had let him clear his mind. He liked that about her.

"Maybe a little Kenny wouldn't be so bad," he said to himself as he drove back across town in his Range Rover, which he picked up from Sunshine's, leaving his Charger there. He stopped at McDonald's and bought breakfast for him and Aida. He was able to make it back before Aida had made it out of bed. Kenny spent the remainder of the day with his wife, and in between, he caught bits of rest before he did a few lines of cocaine and went to work.

KICK DOORS

There was a memorial at the Sunset Police Station for the slain Detective Sam Garboski. O'Brien made his detectives do their best to make Sam look as though he had died under cover in the line of duty and not picking up hookers like he was. The last thing he needed was for the IA to think or know his officers were involved in illegal activities, so Sam was buried with honors. Then O'Brien pushed all assignments back a week and demanded someone be brought to justice for Garboski's murder.

A week later, at 1:45 p.m., the front door of Cyco's big house on L Avenue went flying off its hinges.

"What the fuck, cuzz?" a man lying on a couch asked. Danny Zamora held a pump-action riot shotgun in his face. The sleeping man tried to wipe the cold out of his eyes.

"Keep your hands where I can see them!" Danny screamed behind his riot mask. Kenny ran in next, keyed up off two lines of crystal meth, wearing a riot mask, and armed with an AR-15 assault rifle. Jenny Hall and Ricky Gomez, who were followed by Tamino Sanches, all armed with rifles and shotguns, followed him. The group moved as one through the house, leaving Danny to stand guard of the awestruck gangster on the couch. Kenny led the group high right, Tamino went high left and wide down the dark hallway, while Ricky and Jenny moved low left and right between the both of them. The lights on the end of their rifles shone bright, illuminating the dark hallway. Ricky spotted a swift movement out of the corner of his eye and followed it.

"Freeze! Sunset PD! Come out peacefully, and you won't get hurt," Ricky ordered. His words were met with ten rounds from a 9 mm Smith and Wesson.

"Hold your positions," Kenny ordered, knowing they were protected by their reinforced steel Kevlar vest. The task force took aim on the dark room and opened fire, spraying the room full of automatic rounds. The triggerman dove for cover behind his bed. He hid with his head to the ground until the shooting stopped, then he got to his feet, dropping the pistol. He ran and dove headfirst through a large glass window in the bedroom. When the shooter went flying through the glass window into the backyard, Kenny spun on his heels and ran back down the vacant hallway into the living room. Kenny threw down his rifle and continued to run out of the house. The unsuspecting gunman was running top speed across the front lawn, out of the backyard, when Kenny blindsided him with a flying tackle. The two men fell to the grass, rolling, with Kenny coming up on top, pounding in the man's face.

Tamino and Ricky ran after Kenny and hauled him off the bleeding man, who now was in need of reconstructive plastic surgery.

"Man, that muthafucka just tried to kill us. Fuck that, let me go!" Kenny screamed, pulling his arms from Tamino and Ricky's grasp and ripped off his raid mask so that he could breathe better. Kenny put his hand on his head to try to calm down. His attention locked onto a 2005 Chevy Avalanche cruising down the street. Kenny recognized the truck, but before he could remember where he had seen it, the driver's side window came down, and he looked right into the eyes of Ned "BadLuck" Davis. Kenny nodded his head to the man who wore a look of shock, awe, and betrayal. Kenny knew he had been made. All he had to do was take BadLuck down and protect his identity, but he was already high on some bullshit crystal, and he did not feel like it. Instead, he gave Ned a pass, thinking they would have him soon enough for the BS killings involving Yo Yo Jenkins. Kenny shifted his focus back to the task at hand and helped the team search the house for contraband. They seized two kilograms of powder cocaine and two pounds of weed. They found seven guns and towed two trucks and a lowrider.

Down the street on L Avenue, Darryl, John, and Nicole kicked off the second raid on the home of Cyco, blasting down the house's front door and charging into the living room with a battering ran. Once the room was secure, they proceeded toward the bedroom. As they got closer, they could hear slow music, Jamie Foxx's "Can I Take You Home." John opened the bedroom door and saw Cyco and a naked woman were entwined on top of a big wooden waterbed.

John fired a warning shot into the rooms ceiling. Cyco, startled by the explosion from John's shotgun, jumped up and dove for his side of the bed, leaving the girl to fend for herself. Nicole ran into the room, grabbed the stark-naked girl off the bed, and put her in flex-cuffs.

"Be careful, he may have a gun," Darryl called after her. Cyco popped up from behind the bed with a TEC-9 he kept under the bed frame and sprayed off rounds toward the bedroom door. The detectives took cover in the hallway while Nicole pushed the girl down on the floor and drew her Glock 17 from her hip holster and popped off six shots into the wooden bed frame, bustin' open the waterbed. Two of the bullets tore through the wood frame and into his abdomen. Cyco held the gun in his right hand and grabbed the ripped open flesh of his abdomen in his left.

"Awe, shit, cuzz, this bitch shot me!" he screamed, seeing his blood mixing with the flowing water from the waterbed. He stuck the TEC-9 over the bed frame and sprayed ten rounds toward Nicole, who dove to the floor out of the way. Darryl came back into the room, led by his M-16; he hit Cyco in the right shoulder, spinning him around. Cyco dropped the gun and fell to the wet carpet.

"Fred!" Darryl called Cyco by his first name. "Just give it up. We have the place surrounded."

"Man, fuck that, cuzz, I ain't going back to Sunset Lasey," he said, thinking of the prison madhouse. Cyco picked up the TEC-9 from the soaked carpet where it had fallen from his hand and sprayed off the remaining fourteen rounds in the gun's magazine. Darryl and John took cover again.

"Did you see that? He has a TEC-9. I counted at least thirty-one rounds. We gotta get him now before he reloads," John said, running into the bedroom, and Darryl chased after him. John jumped over the wooden bed frame and crashed down on top of Cyco. He took the back of his pump-action riot shotgun stock and struck Cyco in the head, knocking him unconscious. Darryl put a pair of flex-cuffs on both of the bleeding unconscious man's wrist and dragged him from the room while Nicole escorted his screaming sex partner to the living room. When Cyco was taken to the hospital, the task force searched the house and recovered two police-issued bulletproof vest, one AK-47, three hundred thousand in cash, and one kilogram of rock cocaine.

After the successful raids, the two teams returned to the Sunset police department. While the office was busy and buzzing processing the Sunset Neighborhood Crips and seized evidence, Kenny slipped out of the office and walked around the corner to where he had the '96 Impala parked. He felt enough time had passed where he could turn in the car without raising any suspicions. The same young kid was on duty with his head stuck in an Ironman comic. Kenny noticed he did not take his eyes off the book as he signed the Impala back in and put the keys on the counter. He turned the corner, pulled out his coke tube, and snorted a good helping up his nose. After he got his fix, Kenny rounded the corner of the car return lot and ran smack into Internal Affairs agent Audra Solis.

"Oh my god, I'm sorry, Detective Lake," she said in her country twang.

"It's all right," he said, grabbing her by the elbow so that she could regain her balance.

"Detective Lake, are you off the clock?" she asked, looking into Kenny's eyes. Kenny smiled to himself, knowing she knew like he did that O'Brien promised to let them all off early after the raid.

"I will be soon. Why? What's crackin'?" he asked.

"Because I have a few questions for you," she said.

Kenny looked for a way to turn this situation in his favor. "On or off the record?" Kenny asked with a smile.

"On the record, of course, Detective," she said, blushing.

"Well, I gotta go finish my report from a raid, and I'm off at 12:00 a.m. You wanna get some coffee or something?" he asked, checking his watch.

"Sure, that will be fine," she said.

"All right, I'll meet you in the parking lot at 12:05," he said.

"I'll see you then, Detective Lake," she said, walking away seductively all the way to her car.

Kenny walked back into the office and sat down at his desk to write his report on the Sunset NHC Gang house. Kenny filled out paper after paper with details, then he took the files to Sergeant Steven Dooner.

"Kenny, take a seat," the sergeant said while he wrapped up a phone conversation he was having when Kenny walked in. Kenny sat down and waited until the sergeant lowered the phone's receiver to its cradle. "We're sending you into the Montoya operation this week. We've developed your cover. We have you posing as a freelancer gun for hire and street import exporter," he briefed Kenny.

"But how do I get in? I can't just walk up to him on the street and say, 'Hey, I'm a hustler, let me hustle for and witcha'," Kenny said.

"I know. That's why I'm sending you and Darryl into Club Destiny." Kenny knew the place well. The Montoya strip club was the hottest skin pit in Sunset. "Darryl will be your backup, as your right-hand man. We will have Danny inside as a bartender to get you your weapons. Nicole and Jenny will also be inside, posing as strippers," Steven said.

"I'm going to meet with Agent Solis later this morning," Kenny said, shifting subject.

"What? Why?" the sergeant asked, confused.

"She asked me. I don't know, but I intend to find out," he said, getting up from his chair.

"Don't forget to focus, Kenny, and don't give her anything," the sergeant advised.

Kenny walked out of the sergeant's office and went back to his desk. He opened his desk drawer, making sure no one was watching, then he opened his stash box. Seeing the Desert Eagle made him wish he had took down Ned "BadLuck" Davis so he could plant the gun and get it off his person and business. He dug into the stash box in his desk and pulled out two pills of ex. He picked the cell phone up from his desk and checked his voice mail. There were fifteen messages in total, mostly from Aida and Sunshine. He let the messages play as he closed his drawer.

"Kenny, I just called to say I love you and thanks for last night. It was wonderful," Aida's first message said.

Sunshine's messages were all pretty much the same: "Kenny, I'm bored." He skipped to the next one. "Kenny, I'm tired." Skip. "Kenny, I went shopping and scratched the Range." Skip. "Kenny, the Z needs a tune-up." Skip. "Are you coming over? I love you." Kenny played the last of the messages as he got up from his desk and walked out of the office to the parking lot where he saw the agent waiting with her back turned to him. He closed the phone and walked up behind the unsuspecting agent.

"Lookin' for me?" he said, laughing.

"Actually, I was," she smiled. The pair headed off to Kenny's midnight-blue 2006 Ford Mustang GT on twenty-two-inch chrome MOMOs. Audra got into the passenger seat while Kenny got behind the wheel. He started the car and took off at max speed out of the parking lot. He shifted gears with a fury down Avenger Avenue until he reached his favorite café Duke's on Hunter Lane.

He and Audra sat in a booth by the window and ordered two slices of apple pie and two cups of coffee. Kenny stared into her dark-blue eyes across the table as they ate and drank their cups of coffee. When their plates were removed, Kenny had their cups refilled.

"So, Agent Solis, how does a country woman like you get a name like Solis?" he asked, opening up small talk.

The agent smiled. "We don't have to be so formal, Kenny. You can call me Audra. To answer your question, my father's name is Hector Solis, but more importantly is why I asked you for this meeting Kenny," she said.

"This ought to be good," Kenny said, dripping with sarcasm.

"All right then, Kenny, have you ever accepted illegal money?" she asked.

Kenny broke out in uncontrollable laughter. "You mean, am I on the take? Are you serious? You've gotta be kidding me. Of course not," he lied.

"Have you ever used drugs, assaulted, or murdered anyone outside of the law?" she questioned.

"Well, Ms. Audra, there's all sorts of gray areas in our profession, but I've never crossed the line," he said, not liking her line of questioning.

"Kenny, you have a large amount of money in your bank account—we've checked—an exquisite house, and expensive cars well above a homicide detective's salary. How are all these things legally funded?" she asked, pulling out an ink pen from her suit pocket and a small pocketbook. She tried to read him as his mind scrambled for covers to hide behind.

"I invest in a lot of stocks, and when my favorite Aunt Patty died, she left me a lot of money and property." He paused while Audra scribbled down something on her notepad. *I don't like this smug, conservative bitch, but she looks good as a muthafucka,* he thought. "Is that all?" he asked.

"Yes, that will be all, thank you. I hope you don't feel uncomfortable," she said.

"Naw, you're just doing your job," he said.

"Excuse me, I have to go to the bathroom. I'll be right back," she said, getting up from the table and walking to the bathroom. When Audra went to the bathroom, Kenny went into his pocket, pulled out the two ecstasy pills, and dropped the pills into her coffee. *I'll teach this nosey bitch,* Kenny thought.

Audra walked into the bathroom and went into a stall. She locked the door and pulled her cell phone out her pocket and called her partner, Agent Peter Chan. "Yeah, Peter, I have him here. I'll keep him busy. Proceed as planned," she said, hanging up the phone.

Agent Peter Chan walked into the Sunset police station and went straight to Kenny's desk. He tore through all of Kenny's case files with negative results. He went through his desk, pulling them completely out, and noticed one of the drawers had a wooden false back to it. He opened up the drawer's stash box and located Kenny's stash of ecstasy and the Desert Eagle he took off Yo Yo's person the night he was murdered.

Peter seized the drugs and gun, placing them both in evidence bags. He cleaned up, returned the drawers, and headed to Darryl Johnson's desk. Audra finished her cup of coffee without noticing the mickey. She started to feel the effects of the ex. She took off her right shoe and sent her foot into Kenny's crotch under the table. Kenny laughed inside as Audra could not sit still. She pulled her hair out of her tight bun and ran her fingers through her hair. She felt as though her body was in the middle of a raging inferno.

"You wanna get out of here?" Kenny asked with a sly smile.

"I thought you would never ask," she said, running her hands under her skirt and biting her bottom lip.

Kenny drove the Mustang at top speed, like he was in a Formula 1 race, off down Hunter Lane. He left the café parking lot smoking and blew to the Sunset Motel on Avenger Avenue. He tried his best to focus on the road as Audra kissed and licked his neck, ear, and cheek. Audra could barely contain herself as Kenny paid for the room. Once Kenny got the horny agent into their room, she peeled out of her clothes and underwear like a kid tearing open gifts on Christmas. He took a moment to savor the glorious sight of Audra without clothes. He had imagined she would look good naked by the way her tight suits hugged her curves.

Audra sat down on the end of the bed. She let her hair fall over her shoulder onto her firm, large breast. She spread her legs and smiled at Kenny slyly. She put her hands on both of her thighs and started to giggle.

Kenny and Audra had rough, kinky sex until sunrise. When Audra woke up next to Kenny, she flew into a panic. She did not feel like herself, and everything after the café was a complete disaster, trying to remember. She did think Kenny was attractive in an odd way, but she had not planned on being intimate with him. She was a professional, and sleeping with someone she was building a case against was totally unprofessional.

While Kenny was still asleep, Audra went to work. After all, she was still trying to nail him. She went through his pants pockets but found nothing incriminating. She did find two receipts from a flower delivery shop; both receipts had names and addresses on them. She grabbed the receipts and went to find her clothes; she found them on the floor. She bent down to pick them up and felt an uncomfortable soreness in her vagina and anus. Audra was so disgusted with herself. She just got dressed in her clothes and ran out of the room. She thought about reporting what she believed was a drug-induced rape to her superiors, but she knew she would be yanked off the investigation into the Sunset homicide department and Kenny would walk. No, she wanted to bust Kenny herself. She ran to the motel lobby and called a cab to pick her up.

6

INSIDE CLUB DESTINY

At the week's end, Kenny woke up with a large smile on his face. Everything was going his way. He had not seen Audra Solis since their Sunset Motel romp. He wasn't worried about her reporting him or calling rape because, after all, it did appear to everyone in the café that they were on a date, and he knew they would make credible witnesses.

Sunshine was asleep next to him. He got out of the bed, took a shower, and got dressed in the same clothes that he wore the day before. He did a long line of cocaine, got into his scuffed-up Range Rover, and headed to the eastside of Sunset with haste. Kenny was due to go under cover later that day. At home, he lay in bed with his wife for a few hours and dozed off to sleep. When Kenny woke, back up he went to the closet. He opened his safe, twisting in the three-digit combination. He pulled out ten thousand in cash and gave it to his wife.

"Take this and go shopping for you and the baby," he said, watching Aida's eyes brighten.

"Thank you, baby," she said, wrapping her arms around the back of his neck, kissing him.

"I'm going deep undercover for a while, so things may get a little crazy. I might not be home a few nights or days," he said, pulling away from her kiss. He saw her eyes darken and her face sadden. "Don't be like that, Aida," he said, kissing her back.

She smiled. "I know. I just hate when you are gone. I miss you, and I worry about you," she confided.

"I know, I know, but I gotta get us paid, baby, so don't trip. Go out, take care of yourself, hit up a spa or something. I gotta go to the cleaners. I'll holler at you later," he said, kissing her again and leaving the room.

Kenny left his house at 12:30 p.m. and went to Lei Wong Cleaners to pick up his tux for the evening. When he went back home, Aida was already gone. He was still feeling the effects from the night before he passed out and went back into a deep slumber. When he woke up again, it was 5:40 p.m., and he felt rejuvenated. He got out of bed and went to take a shower; he got dressed in the tuxedo, putting on a pair of white Stacy Adams to match his white undershirt, vest, and suit. Then he did a line of speed just to get himself really going. Kenny checked himself over in a full-length mirror. "I look like a million bucks," he said to himself before he left the house, headed for the station.

Kenny arrived at the Sunset police department at 7:40 p.m. He walked into Steven Dooner's office, and Darryl was already there, dressed in a white two-piece suit. He had shaved off all his facial hair too.

"You look gay and happy as a fag in a dick tree," he said to his partner. He hated when Darryl shaved his face.

"Man, fuck you," Darryl said.

When Tamino Sanches and John walked into the office, the sergeant closed the door and started a four-hour briefing. At the end of the meeting, Kenny knew all there was to know about the Montoya operation, how they got their drugs in from TJ into the gates, and all the murders they were charged with and beat.

"Lake! Johnson! You'll need these too," the sergeant said, tossing two envelopes across the table to them as Tamino fitted them for an undetectable mic that went under their clothes. "It's ten large a piece. Remember, get Umberto to notice you, throw a little money around if need be. Danny's already in, working the bar. He has your weapons.

Once we get in the cartel, we're good as gold. Let's do it, team," the sergeant said, concluding the meeting.

Kenny and Darryl pulled to a stop in front of Club Destiny in the back of a white stretched Hummer limo. There was a crowd of Mexican men standing out front trying to get into the club. Their attention quickly shifted to the two black men with flashy jewelry and fancy suits getting out of the big Hummer. The two detectives made their way over to the front door and got stopped short by the two big Mexican bouncers watching the door. Kenny looked up at the big man standing before him at six foot five, rounding off at 230 pounds. The man standing in front of Darryl was a tad bit smaller at six foot four, 200 pounds.

"What chu want, maine?" the door guard asked in a thick Hispanic accent.

"We want to spend our money, maine!" Kenny said, pulling a stack of bills from his pocket and waved them in the guard's face.

"Turn around so we can pat you down," the guard said just as Kenny knew he would. After all, money did talk in Sunset. Both Kenny and Darryl did as they were instructed and held their arms out to their sides so the door guards could search them for weapons. As Kenny faced out to the street, he saw John and Tamino driving by in a black surveillance van and park down the road.

"All right, ya'll are clean. You can go in," the bigger of the two guards said, holding out his palm for the fifty-dollar admission fee. Kenny gave the man three fifties and told him to keep the change. The guard stepped out of the way and let them in the club.

When they both walked into Club Destiny, they saw naked and half-naked women all around them, dancing and passing out drinks. Kenny looked at the club's layout. It was simple enough. The bottom level consisted of a mirrored stage with three gold stripper poles, one in the center and two off to the sides. Tables filled with patrons surrounded the stage. There was a long bar off to the right of the club. Kenny saw Danny serving drinks, then he looked up at the large balcony overlooking the bottom level of the club. Kenny picked out a table where he could be viewed by all when they wanted to be seen.

"Wait here, I'll go get the heat," Kenny said loudly over the throbbing sounds of the house music. Kenny strolled over to the big bar and sat on a stool. Danny Zamora walked in front of him. "Can I get you something?" he asked Kenny, looking around at the other bartender to see if they were paying them any attention, but no one was.

"Let me get two bottles of Moet and them thizzles," Kenny said, putting $200 in cash on the bar. Danny reached into the small of his back, looking over both shoulders to make sure the coast was clear, and handed Kenny a .25 semiautomatic pistol, then he handed him one bottle of Moet. Kenny stuffed the .25 in his vest pocket. Danny went into his back pocket, pulled out a six-shot .22 Ruger and handed it to Kenny in a napkin, then he gave him the other bottle of Moet. Kenny put the revolver in the pocket of the inside of his suit, picked up the second bottle of Moet, and headed back to his table.

Kenny sat down and handed Darryl a bottle of the champagne, then he fished the revolver out of his inside pocket and handed it to his partner. "Keep it in the small of your back in case they pat us down again. You ready, Dee?" he asked.

"Yup," he said, putting the gun into his waistband.

"All right, here we go," he said, opening his bottle of Moet and putting the bottle to his lips. He turned it up. The club's music lowered, and the DJ's voice came over the loudspeaker.

"Pimps, playas, and playa haters, we got us something new jumpin' off foe us tonight. Her name is Keesha Rue, and she's working her way through the University of Sunset College. She's from our west side, and she's an aspiring actress. Ya'll put your hands together for Ms. K-Rue," he announced. There was a round of applause as Detective Nicole Brown took the stage. R. Kelly's slow wind blasted out of the club's speakers. Nicole started to dance slowly, stripping off her overshirt and tossing it into the front row, onto an excited onlooker. She was grinding her hips while she undid her skirt; she let it fall to her ankles and kicked it across the stage. Then she ran and jumped on the pole. The crowd went crazy as she spun around it. The stage was filling with dollar bills. She peeled out of her bra top, exposing her breasts, and then she dropped to her hands and knees and crawled to the end of the stage in front of Kenny as the song ended. She turned around putting her ass in his face, bouncing it up and down, wiggling it back and forth, left to right. Kenny threw several bills at her backside. She ran her thumbs around her G-string, taking it off and tossing it to him. Kenny smiled as he watched Nicole bend over at the waist at the end of the song, giving him a full view of her goodies. At the end of the song, she gathered up all the money on the stage, shot him a look, and flipped her head back, tossing her long, black hair down her back as she exited the stage.

"Damn, she was good, Dee," he said to Darryl.

"Yeah, too good," Darryl said as if he was angry. Kenny shot him a confused look. *Another time,* he thought. He did not have time to see what was bugging Darryl.

Kenny took the twenty-five out of his vest pocket and put it into his waistband before he started to pay for lap dances and throw more money on the stage. Darryl started to get in on the action, tossing his money around on the stage and buying lap dances. Kenny got louder and louder, jumped on top of the table, and ordered drinks around the stage. Kenny looked up to the balcony and saw Umberto Montoya looking down at him. Kenny grabbed a girl walking by with a tray full of drinks in her hand.

"Take my friend up there a bottle of Moet," he said, pointing at Umberto. "Tell him it's from Cody and Max." He put a hundred dollar bill and a twenty on her tray and gave her a pat on the butt. "Keep the change." He winked.

Kenny watched her as she went to the bar, got a bottle of Moet and a glass, and ran it upstairs to Umberto in the VIP section. Umberto took the glass and bottle from the girl and poured the bubbling beverage into the glass. He raised it in the air to Kenny and Darryl in salute. Kenny and Darryl raised their glasses back in return. They sat back down and continued to pour money into the Montoya establishment.

Umberto Montoya had been watching Kenny and Darryl off and on since they walked into his club. He could smell money a mile away, and these two were loaded. He also liked the show his new girl had put on. K-Rue had made a lot of money for herself. He thought about promoting her to VIP. He watched the two young black men continue to spend money like water. He thought about bringing them up to the high-roller section and let them gamble and play with his personal women. What money did they come from? he wondered as he saw the man in the white suit with the big diamond earrings grabbed one of his girls, whispered into her ear, and sent her to bring him a bottle of his most expensive champagne. He signaled a toast to the two men and drank down the Moet. He had seen enough and made up his mind.

"Rodamez, Santino, Carlos!" Umberto shouted over the loud music. The three men came running to the screaming cartel don. Umberto could sense an air of annoyance in his brother's face. He knew his younger brother hated doing his bidding. "Go bring those two black men in the white suits up here to VIP," he ordered.

Kenny and Darryl were busy tossing money onto the stage at Jenny Hall, posing as a stripper going by the name of Goldie, when the three Mexican men approached them. "Stand up, Boss wants to see you two," Carlos said.

Kenny and Darryl stood up and looked at the trio. Kenny recognized the man standing behind Carlos as Rodamez Montoya. Carlos and Santino patted them down with negative results and lead them upstairs to the VIP section of the club. The VIP section of the club was a whole new world in comparison to the rest of the club. The top floor was covered with couches and soft large chairs for lap dancing and sexual acts. On the other side of the room was a big crap table, a pool table, and two poker tables. There were two doors set off to the side of the pool table—one said Bathroom; the other one was unmarked. There was several men and women engaged in sexual activities on the couches, while every table had gamblers.

"Welcome, my friends," Umberto said, greeting Kenny and Darryl with an extended hand. Both detectives shook hands with the drug lord. "I am Umberto, and this is my little brother, Rodamez. Welcome to VIP of Club Destiny," he said, pointing to Rodamez then twirling around to indicate the top floor of the club.

"My name is Maxamillion, but I go by Max, and this is my comrade, Cody Wayman," Kenny said. As Kenny made his introduction, he noticed Rodamez was not as impressed or as inviting as his brother was.

"Now that is out of the way, what's your game, gentlemen?" Umberto asked.

Kenny walked over and sat down in the one vacant chair available at the poker table. "It's one thousand a hand," the dealer said.

Good, Kenny thought, looking at the man across from him with the big ten-gallon hat, big buckle on his belt, and pointed boots. The Mexican didn't look like he played poker a day in his life. The other three men did. They, like himself, were dressed in fancy suits and reeked of illegal money.

They started to play, and Kenny was doing all right, then he started to do good. Maybe a little too good, because he raised his pot to fifteen grand, and he saw the dealer slide an ace out of his sleeve to trump his straight flush with a royal flush. Kenny excused himself to the bathroom. Once he was alone, he cut off the wire communications with John and Tamino. He didn't need Tamino recording what he intended on doing.

When Kenny returned to his seat, he cashed out for two thousand of his own money. The fifteen was the money of the other gamblers and a grand of his own. He watched the dealer perform his shifty dealings as he pulled earlier. Kenny loaded up with a straight flush again; he watched the dealer's hands as he dealt the kick outs. Kenny didn't want any cards. He raised the pot up a full grand, the other three men at the table all folded except for the dealer, who met Kenny's raise and called. Kenny grabbed the table and flipped it upside-down, sending money and chips flying all over the place.

He pulled the pistol out of his waistband in a flash and held it to the dealer's skull. Darryl, Carlos, Santino, and Rodamez all pulled their guns and pointed them at each other.

"Help me," the dealer whimpered.

"This muthafucka has been cheating me all game. He has the fuckin' cards up his shirt sleeve," Kenny said to Umberto while he strode over and grabbed the dealers right arm and pulled two aces and two kings from his shirt sleeve.

"Lower your weapons," Umberto said, counting the cards. Carlos, Santino, and Darryl all put their sidearms back in their waistbands. Rodamez still held his .45 on Kenny, and Kenny still held his .25 on the dealer. "Rodamez, I said put it away!" the don shouted at his little brother. Rodamez frowned and shoved the pistol down the front of his pants. "Max, go ahead and put that down, maine, we'll take care of this," he said. Kenny put the gun back into the back of his waistband and let the dealer go. "Carlos, Santino, take this man out back," Umberto ordered.

The two guards grabbed the dealer and escorted him out back. Being beaten by Umberto's brow of fury for letting the two black men into his establishment in his state of rage, Umberto made an irrational decision outside of his beliefs. "Max, Cody, what is your business? What do you do for work?" he asked.

"We're into import export—anything you need in Sunset, we can get it," Kenny said.

"Well, come by tomorrow morning. We may be able to do some business," Umberto said, walking to the door at the side of the pool table and disappearing inside. Kenny and Darryl walked out of Club Destiny and got back into the stretched Hummer.

"Ya'll get that? We are all in," Darryl said to John and Tamino over his wire.

Damn, Kenny thought. He had forgotten about Tamino's connection to Darryl's wire when he clipped his own. He leaned back in the limo and checked his voice mail. There was a message from Aida and two from Sunshine.

"Kenny, the Internal Affairs came by the house twice tonight. What do you want me to do?" Aida asked.

"Kenny, call or come see me right away. It's urgent," Sunshine said on her first message. "Fuck it, Kenny, I'm pregnant," she said.

Kenny looked down at the phone in his hand and frowned with mixed emotions of confusion, disappointment, and frustration. He did not know which message was worse. He hung up the phone. His mind was going in a million different directions at once.

7

UNDER INVESTIGATION

It was around 12:45 p.m. when Kenny was able to get out of bed. He took a quick shower and got dressed in a black-and-red Air Jordan jumpsuit. When he came home the night before, Aida was already asleep. He made it home just before sunrise, so he let her sleep. She wasn't in bed when he woke up. Aida was out in the pool, enjoying a swim. He let his mind race a hundred miles per hour as he made himself a bowl of instant oatmeal. His thoughts drifted to the IA and Agent Audra Solis and the sex they had. He knew he should have just left her alone, but he just could not control himself.

Kenny finished his oatmeal and dropped his bowl and spoon into the sink as he walked into the backyard. Aida was busy sunbathing on a floating inner tube when Kenny came into the backyard. Aida's eyes were closed as she floated on the crystal blue water.

"Aida! Aida!" Kenny shouted, snapping her out of her trance. She lifted her neck and shot an I-don't-want-to-be-bothered look his way. "Aida, I need to talk to you," he said, looking at her body, glistening from the water from the pool and beads of sweat from the heat of the blistering sun overhead.

Aida put her head back on the raft and closed her eyes again. "Later, baby, I'm relaxing," she said.

What? Kenny thought. "This is a matter of freedom or jail. I need to speak with you," he said, watching the raft carry his wife closer to the poolside.

"All right, Kenny, go ahead, I'm listening," she said with her eyes still closed. Kenny looked at his glistening wife and felt himself being aroused. *Control yourself and focus,* he told himself.

His rage took over. This was a serious matter, and Aida didn't even get out to see what he was talking about, he thought. Kenny reach down into the pool just as the raft reached the railing and grabbed Aida by the wrist, pulling her off the raft then up onto the pool ledge before him.

"Kenny, what the fuck?" she exclaimed, her sore wrist still in his hand.

"I said we need to talk," he said, watching his wife's eyes go to the bulge growing in his pants. She threw herself against him, trying to kiss him. Kenny pulled away from her. "Naw, girl, I need to know what happened with Internal Affairs."

"Let go of my wrist, Kenny, you're hurting me," she said, starting to cry.

Fuck, I ain't got time for all this emotional shit, he thought, releasing his grip on her wrist. "What did the IA tell you or ask you?" Kenny asked as he started interrogating his wife.

"The first time I was coming back from shopping for the baby when this Asian man got out this car and walked up to me. He showed me a badge and handed me a card and said, 'I'm with the Internal Affairs,'" she shared.

"You still have the card?" he asked.

"Yeah, it's in the house on the coffee table," she said.

"What happened next?" he asked.

"He asked if you were doing drugs, and I said no. He asked if you had any firearms that weren't registered, and I said no. He asked if you were taking any kind of illegal money, and I said no. Then he asked to search the house, and I said no, not without a search warrant," she said.

"You did good. Anything else?" he asked.

"The second time he came, I called you. He asked the same questions. The third time he came, he was just looking around the house from the outside," she said.

"The third time?" Kenny screamed, running back into the house. He ran into the bedroom and searched his closet. After he didn't find what he was looking for, Kenny dropped to his knees in front of the glass nightstand next to their bed. He ran his fingers down the bottom of the iron railings until he felt the small black transmitter.

"What's the matter, Kenny? What are you looking for? Are you in some kind of trouble?" Aida asked, walking into the bedroom.

"Fuck, we've been bugged. The next time these police of police come back, they will have a search warrant," he said to his wife, getting up from the floor and walking into the bathroom to flush the bug down the toilet. He ran through the rest of the house, looking for more bugs. He found one in every room and disposed of them.

"I'll be back. I got to try and get this shit under control, baby, I'll call you later," he said, leaving in his Ford Mustang, heading for Sunshine's house. Kenny needed peace. He couldn't get it at home with Aida, so he sped to see his mistress. He almost crashed into a big rig as he swooped illegally around the truck. When he arrived at the apartment, Kenny busted into the living room, searching the whole unit for the Internal Affair's bugs. When he was convinced there were none, he relaxed some. Sunshine looked at him like he was crazy.

Kenny walked into the kitchen and poured a small pile of cocaine from a sugar pot he kept on the counter onto a glass plate. He went and sat down on the couch and put the plate on the coffee table and pulled a bankroll of bills from his pocket. He rolled up a hundred dollar bill, put one end of the makeshift straw to his nose, the other end to the plate, and inhaled the white powder into his nose. He sat the plate down on the table and leaned back on the couch, resting his head in Sunshine's lap. She caressed his head as he looked up into her eyes.

"Kenny, I'm pregnant, and we're not married. My baby needs a father," she said, starting to sob.

"That's why you have to have an abortion, baby. You know I can't leave her now. She's my wife, and she's having my baby too. If you won't let me take care of you and the baby from my life with Aida and my family, you gotta get an abortion," he said, closing his eyes.

Sunshine exploded in a rage, attacking Kenny, hitting him in the face, and digging her nails in his face and chest. Kenny grabbed her by both arms and slid off the couch to his feet. He wrapped his arms around her arms and mid torso, tossed her onto the couch, and walked out of the apartment.

"Kenny, stop! Come back! Talk to me!" she screamed after him as he slammed the door shut.

Kenny walked over to Sunshine's 2004 Nissan Z. He got in the car, started it up, and burned rubber out of the apartment parking lot and headed to Club Destiny so that he could meet with Umberto Montoya.

When Kenny stepped out of Sunshine's apartment, two flashes went off from a high-tech camera that Agent Peter Chan aimed from the back seat of his small Honda Civic hatchback. The agent sat in plain sight, undetected, even to a trained eye like Kenny's. He took two more pictures of Kenny getting into the metallic-silver-flaked Z as he left speeding out of the parking lot. Peter kept a safe distance from the Z as he followed Kenny weaving in and out of traffic. He parked the car across the street from Club Destiny as Kenny parked by the front door and got out the car. Peter got off two more flashes, then he picked up his cell phone and dialed Audra Solis.

"Hello, Agent Chan here. Lake has just entered a club on Hope Street. I'll report any further changes or occurrences, Chan out," he said, canceling the phone call.

Kenny walked into the club, but Club Destiny had a different look in the day than it did at night. There was several patrons in the business, but it was not rocking like it did in the wee hours of the day. Kenny was met at the front door by Carlos and Santino and searched fully, this time by the two guards. He knew he would be attending this meeting without a weapon because he knew Danny didn't have a shift during the daytime hours.

"I'm clean, man, really," he said.

"No funny shit, this time, maine," Carlos said, giving Kenny a pat on the back. Kenny was escorted upstairs to the VIP section. Kenny noticed a few Mexican men shooting dice at the crap table as he was led to the room on the pool table's side. It served as Umberto's office.

The inside of Umberto Montoya's office was like something out of a mafia don movie. There was a large desk made out of marble in the center of the room. Behind it sat a large throne-like leather chair, and twenty surveillance monitors sat off to the back against the wall, stacked on top of one another, showing almost every square inch of the club, even the front and the back entrances of the club. The room was lined with big statues of Mayan Aztec warriors, and painted pictures lined the walls. There was a large stretched-out tiger-skin rug in the center of the floor matching the three-seater, brown-and-orange trim leather couch. Kenny could not believe what his eyes were seeing. There had to be a kilogram or more of powder cocaine piled up on top of the marble desk in front of Umberto Montoya, who sat back in his chair with white powder on his face.

Rodamez sat off to the side on the couch while Kenny took a seat in one of the two empty brown-and-orange trim chairs in front of his desk. Rodamez shot Kenny a smug I-do-not-like-you-much look, which Kenny returned. Rodamez's face shriveled up like a lemon. Kenny turned his attention to Umberto Montoya, who sat at his desk smiling at him while he rolled up a hundred dollar bill and extended it to Kenny across the coke pile.

"Max, do you use? If so, help ya self, maine," he said.

Kenny took the makeshift straw, put his nose to one end and the other end to the pile, and snorted up a good dose of the drug.

"That's right, my friend, loosen up," Umberto encouraged, laughing. "So, Max, how does a boss of import export operate? How can you help us exactly?" he asked.

"An importer exporter means there is nothing I can't get for you in Sunset City," Kenny said.

Umberto smiled. He liked the black man; he seemed to be confident in his ability. "This is what I'm talking about Rodamez. Good help is hard to find, like Max," he said to his younger brother. Rodamez was not impressed. "A man with your connections could be useful to our business," Umberto said sincerely.

"I agree," Kenny said.

"I'll need you to pass a few tests first, of course," Umberto said.

"No problem," Kenny said.

"Good, come with me. I got something for you," Umberto said, rising from his desk, leading the way out of the office. Kenny followed behind the Montoya cartel men next door to the vacant space of the club. The building was without walls and empty, except for a lone figure of a man slumped in a corner and covered by a suit jacket.

Umberto and Rodamez stopped short of Kenny, letting him and Santino walk over to the Mexican man on the floor. "Go ahead, Max, pull the jacket off," Umberto encouraged.

Kenny had no idea who or what he would find under the jacket, but he lifted it anyway, revealing the Mexican man who cheated him earlier in the card game. The man's hands and feet were bound together; his face was swollen and caked with dry blood from being beaten almost to death.

Santino handed Kenny a .357 Magnum. They all looked at Kenny, waiting. *This is it, this is the test. Awe, shit,* Kenny thought, grabbing the hand cannon, aiming it at the man's face. Without a second thought, Kenny squeezed a round into his forehead, blowing his brains onto his and Santino's shoes, pants, and legs. Murder was second nature to Kenny. Kenny cleaned off as best as he could in the VIP bathroom and agreed to meet with his family later in the week.

When Kenny left Club Destiny, Rodamez sat in a chair in front of his brother's desk. "I don't trust him. Why are you so trusting and putting him in the family business? This is not how we do business," he tried to reason with his older brother.

Umberto was so upset with his brother he threw a notepad across the room. "How dare you question my judgment? I know what is right for us. I know what this family needs. I built this family. I am the Montoya family—I am the boss! Me, not you. You will respect my rules, Rodamez," he said. Rodamez never voiced his opinions to the elder Montoya again in regard to his new pal, Max.

Agent Audra Solis had all the evidence confiscated in relation to the Internal Affairs office. She processed the Desert Eagle and ran it in the computer. The gun came back stolen from the Sunset Hills. After a ballistics test was ran, the gun came back as the murder weapon of two Sunset Neighborhood Crips. Next, she ran the prints on the actual gun. Two sets of prints were on the gun—one was Kenny's, and the other set belonged to Bobby "Yo Yo" Jenkins.

Kenny went in to the office and went to his desk to get his mind in order. The office was mostly empty except for Danny Zamora, which meant Ricky was probably doing his wife. John was busy at his desk, and Darryl was chatting with Tamino in the back of the office. Kenny waved for John to come over. When he came, he sat down at his desk. They hadn't spoken much since the Garboski slaying.

"I just smoked some fool for the Montoya's man. I'm in deep," Kenny said, opening his bottom desk drawer.

"Man, what happen? K, you know the IA been creepin' around here," John said.

"I know. They were just testing me. They gave me some coke and put a gun in my hand. I passed the test with flying colors. The fucking IA had been at my house three times. Check this out," he said, digging into his suit jacket, pulling out a business card from his pocket and handing it to John. He held the card between his index finger and thumb as he read it. "Agent Peter Chan, Internal Affairs."

"Some piece of work, this guy," John said.

"I know," Kenny said, opening the stash spot in the drawer to pop an ecstasy pill, but it was empty. Kenny's face twisted into a frown. "Where is it? Where the fuck is it?" Kenny screamed.

"What is it?" John asked.

"The gun, John, the fuckin' gun is gone!" Kenny shouted, getting up from his chair and walking to the back of the office where Darryl and Tamino were at. John followed him.

"Darryl where is it? Where the fuck is the gun?" Kenny asked.

"What gun?" Darryl asked.

"The gun that was in my desk," he said.

"I don't know, man," he said, getting up from his chair.

"Fuck, they got it," Kenny said.

"Got what?" Tamino asked.

"Nothin', Sanches, don't trip. Ya'll, I'm going in to holler at Dooner," Kenny said, leaving the three men at the back of the office. Kenny exploded into the sergeant's office. Steven was busy with papers on his desk. "We gotta talk," Kenny said, closing the door.

"What's the problem, Lake?" the sergeant asked.

"The fucking IA is the problem. They are fucking all over me, buggin' my house, pestering my wife, and they took a gun and some dope out of my fuckin' desk. Get them off my back, Steve!" Kenny screamed.

"What do you want me to do?" Sergeant Dooner asked.

"What I just said—get them off of me! I just broke into the Montoya cartel. If you don't do something, I'm going to cut loose and flee. Fuck the case, fuck the money, and fuck this team. You get them off me!" he threatened.

"I'll do what I can, Ken," the sergeant promised.

"No, you get it done, Steve, and you better think about why you don't want the IA arresting me. Thought about it yet? Good get it done," Kenny said, walking out of the sergeant's office and out to lunch with his friend John.

INSIDE THE MONTOYAS

After a month of working for the Montoyas, Kenny seemed to still be proving himself to Rodamez, who was always making requests for either him or Darryl to fill. The requests were usually small enough to fill with the help of the department. A few AK-47s here, a couple cases of Moet there, a speedboat for half price, stolen cars to be tagged. Kenny and Darryl were breaking their necks to get the younger Montoya's orders filled, but they never were a disappointment, which brought them deeper into the fold with Rodamez's blessing.

"Max, Cody, if you fuck over the family, I will kill you," he said, hugging both men.

Soon after, Kenny and Darryl were driving the cartel's drugs and bringing them across the border from Mexico to Sunset. At times there would be immigrants they would smuggle in with the dope, but Kenny didn't care as long as he got paid and got the two kilograms they stole every time they did a drop for the Montoyas. They had so much they wouldn't miss two bricks here and there. Kenny never kept anything at home or at his job because of the IA. Instead, he got himself a public storage slot and did his business there. When Kenny was not at the job or driving dope, he was with Umberto. Most of the time, he was soaking up the kingpin's business mind state. Kenny had been undercover a month, and neither him nor Darryl had anything on the Montoya cartel to show O'Brien, so the chief shifted the point to Detective Nicole Brown as lead investigator. She began to stick her nose in everything. She was busy cleaning up glasses and ashtrays from VIP when Umberto and Kenny were discussing business on his couch.

The tan woman caught his eye as he spoke. "Excuse me, Max. Dancer, you in the orange, come in my office!" Umberto shouted. Nicole stopped what she was doing and walked into the office. Both Kenny and Umberto studied her tight body wrapped in the orange bikini top and matching G-string.

"How may I help you?" she asked.

"Uh, what's your name again? I forget," Umberto asked.

"She's K-Rue," Kenny said, smiling.

"Ah yes, yes, Ms. K-Rue, I would like you to come work private dances in the VIP lounge. It will require several sexual acts, but you will make a substantial amount of money. Is this job something you would like to pursue?" he asked.

Nicole shook her head no; she did not want to work in VIP. Instead, she said, "I'm cool on that, Big Papi, but I think it would be better if I worked with you like if we had a business arrangement."

Umberto looked at her with lust in his eyes. He had wanted her since the first night he laid eyes on her. Now he had her. Nicole looked at Kenny with a sense of panic in her eyes, hoping he would do something to prevent her from performing the acts Umberto suggested. She wanted to just leave, but she had been made the lead investigator on the Montoya case, and she did not want to blow her only in with the Montoyas.

She got down on her knees in front of Umberto seated next to Kenny on the couch. She pulled down his pants and went to work pleasing the cartel don. When she topped him off, Umberto pointed to Kenny. "Now him," he directed.

Smug bitch, that's what you get. You wanted to take over the investigation by sucking your way to the top, so suck. You gotta take one for the team, Kenny thought. Looking Nicole square in the eye, he leaned back on the couch and smiled.

"If you gonna do it, do it right. Hit it hard, girl," he said, grabbing the back of her head and guiding her to her work.

Darryl walked into the office just as Nicole was pulling her face off Kenny's lap.

"Hey, Cody, you want to get in on this?" Umberto asked.

"Uh no, I'm good," he said, slightly embarrassed. "I just need to have a word with Max."

Kenny got up from the couch and walked into the VIP lounge with his partner.

"What the fuck are you doing, man?" Darryl shrieked.

"I'm getting some head from Nicole, what it look like I'm doing?" Kenny said, zipping up his fly.

"You're out of line, K. You went too far. What are you going to do when you get reported?" he asked.

"I ain't gonna do nothing 'cause I was doing my job. Now get the fuck out of my face," Kenny answered, pushing Darryl out of the way of his path blocking the stairs. He went downstairs to get a drink at the bar.

Umberto Montoya found himself taken with Detective Nicole Brown so much so they became inseparable. This compromised him as boss of the cartel. Umberto felt so comfortable he continued to do things he would have never done if he were not smitten by the love bug. He conducted several of his business affairs in front of her, and each time, she made sure his men paid. Tamino, John, and Ricky Gomez were able to get a bust, which made her the most productive detective on the case. As the lead detective, she reported Kenny and tried to have him thrown off the case, but Sergeant Steven Dooner refused, saying Kenny was in too deep and pulling him out would jeopardized the whole case. Instead, Kenny was reprimanded and told he would be on a short leash. Kenny had had enough of Nicole and her goodie-two-shoes routine. It was time for her to sing a new tune.

He was on his way to visit his boy Umberto when Nicole and Darryl cut him off in midstride.

"Did you kill a man for the Montoyas?" Nicole asked.

"Huh, what? Where you get that shit from?" Kenny asked.

"The Montoyas are trying to figure out who's the mole. They say it's not you because you killed a man for them off the record and off file. I'm going to have to report this, Kenny. You've went way over deep cover. You're corrupt, and you make me sick," Nicole said.

"Bitch, what?" Kenny said, trying to grab her in the middle of a crowded VIP.

Darryl stepped between the two of them. "Hold up, K," he said, grabbing Kenny by both shoulders.

"Nigga, get yo hands off me. You savin' a ho?" Kenny said, catching Darryl with a right hook to the chin. After the first blow, Darryl threw a hook that connected to Kenny's temple. After both men, exchanged blows, Santino and Carlos grabbed the two men by their arms and separated them.

"Aye, no fighting in the club. Max, come on, maine, Boss wants to see you anyway," Carlos said, leading Kenny back to the office.

Darryl snatched his arms free of Santino's grasp and walked downstairs. Nicole followed him down to the first floor of the club.

"Another fucking shipment just got picked off by the pigs. It's that fucking bitch you keep running your mouth around twenty four seven," Rodamez challenged his older brother.

"What? Wait, no, if anybody is a cop, it's Max or Cody," Umberto said, high on cocaine, trying his best to save his mistress, no matter who he had to throw under the bus.

"When Max first came around, you know I hated him most of all, but fact is fact. Max is no rat. The problems is, you're getting sloppy, old man," Rodamez said as Kenny walked into the office.

"What's going on, Umberto, you wanted to see me?" Kenny asked.

"Oh yes, Max, tell my big brother here that you're no rat," Rodamez said.

"What? Are you kidding me? I can tell you who the rat is, and it's not me or Cody," he said.

"You know who the rat is? How?" Umberto asked.

"It's K-Rue. She's not who she says she is," Kenny said with an arrogant smile.

"How do you know?" Umberto asked.

"Because I saw her driver's license fall out of her purse, and I picked it up and read it. Her name is Nicole Brown, and I can guarantee everything you ever discussed in front of that bitch ended in a police raid," Kenny said, making his case. Rodamez smiled.

It took almost a month for Sergeant Dooner to get a meeting with the Internal Affairs director, James Willis, to get him off Kenny's back. "I need you to keep Agent Solis and Chan off Detective Lake," he said to his old friend.

"Steven, I could lose my job or, worse, do time," the director said.

"I need you to do this for me, James. We're in over our heads. You have to do what I'm asking you to do," he said

"All right, I'll do my best, and more," the director said.

Audra Solis could not believe what she was hearing. She was being denied a search warrant by her supervisor even after all the evidence she presented of misconduct and foul doings on Kenny's behalf. So she took her case to James Willis herself.

"Detective Kenny Lake is slime, sir, a disgrace to the badge and justice. I believe he is participating in murder, rape, extortion, robbery, and narcotics trafficking. We need to get him off the street," she said, handing the director a file.

"I agree this all sounds like he needs to get off the streets, Agent Solis, but the judge has spoken. I will do what I can. In the meantime, stay away from Detective Lake. Do not go anywhere near the Sunset police department or his residence," he said.

"But, sir," Audra protested.

"No buts, Solis. Leave it be," he ordered, feeling like the sellout he was, but he was a man of honor and he owed his life to Steven Dooner, who had taken a bullet for him when they were beat cops.

Audra was beside herself with rage. She looked down at the flower receipt she held in her hand, which she had taken out of Kenny's pants pocket. She knew what she had to do now.

Kenny was feeling better after he had convinced Rodamez to put a hit on "K-Rue." He knew she would not make it through the night, which meant she wouldn't have a chance to report anything about the murder to O'Brien.

He went over to Sunshine's and worked out an agreement that he would raise her kid with her as a second family. He could afford it with the money him, Darryl, John, and Steven Dooner were making off the Montoya operation.

Detective Nicole Brown left the club after her shift. She got in her burgundy four-door '86 Cutlass and drove to her condo across town. When she got out of her car to make the trot from the curb to the complex, two large Mexican men in all black came from behind a blue van and approached her. One man grabbed her by the neck and put her in a chokehold while the other man took a hold of her feet and legs, hauling her into the van.

It was extremely cold in Umberto Montoya's mansion. The sun was yet to rise, and a light rain had begun to fall. His mood was gloomy, and he hated bad weather. He laid awake in bed next to his wife, Maria. He wished his wife weren't home, and he could have Keesha in bed with him instead. He pulled the cover up to his neck, figuring he would spend the whole day in bed. He started to doze back off to sleep when his bedroom door flew open and two gunmen ran to the foot of his bed armed with two TEC-9's.

Umberto rolled over in bed, clutching the cover as though it were a shield. "What the fuck?" were the only words he was able to utter before the gunmen cut loose with over fifty-five rounds into the helpless don and his sleeping wife.

Kenny arrived at Club Destiny in a so-so mood, half because it was early and half because he didn't know what he was being summoned for. He came in and went straight to the VIP and into the office to find Umberto. When he walked through the door, Rodamez turned around in the big swivel chair Umberto usually sat in.

"How ya' doin', Maxie?" Rodamez said in a good mood.

"Where is Umberto? I thought he wanted to see me," Kenny said.

"He checked out early for the day," the younger Montoya said. "We're under new management now. Come with me, Max, I got something I want to show you." Rising from the chair, Rodamez led Kenny next door to the same vacant building where he had shot the card cheat.

When the men arrived in the building, Kenny found Detective Nicole Brown stripped nude, whipped, gagged, and bound at the wrist to a small steam pipe above her head. Her eyes were filled with fear until she saw Kenny. She started to wiggle and shake her head, begging him for help with her eyes.

"You were right, Max. This bitch is a fucking rat. We got into her locker and went in her purse. The bitch had a fucking shield. She's a Sunset police officer, maine," he said, pulling a knife out of his pocket. He opened up the blade and grabbed her breast one by one, cutting off her hardened nipples.

Nicole felt searing pain as the steel blade ripped through her flesh. She screamed out against her gag.

"You want to say something, princess?" Rodamez asked, mocking her before he stabbed her over thirty times in the chest, abdomen, and back until she went into shock and bled out.

"Maxie, grab that ax in the corner," he said. Kenny walked over to the corner and picked up the ax. He walked to where Nicole's hanging corpse was slouched over the pipe by her wrist restraints.

Rodamez reached over the hanging corpse with his knife and cut her down, the body dropping to the floor in a heap. "Good. Give me the ax and straighten her out so I can cut her up," Rodamez directed. Kenny rolled Nicole onto her back and spread her arms out, then he spread her legs apart and looked at Rodamez, who was smiling from ear to ear. "You ever chop up a body, Max?" he asked. Kenny shook his head no. "I'll do half, you do the other half. Hold the leg in place so it don't move," Rodamez said, bringing the ax back and then forward, chopping off the body's right foot at the ankle. "See, it's all about the joints, Max," he said, cutting off the right femur at the knee.

Kenny almost hurled but managed to keep it together as Rodamez kept chopping the hands, arms, thighs, biceps, the head, and the neck. He handed the bloody ax to Kenny. "She's all yours, maine," he said, laughing. Kenny took the dulling ax and cut off the foot, then a part of the leg, then he threw up.

"Ooh, Max, here. Give me the ax. I got it, maine," he said, laughing.

Even though the Internal Affairs director, James Willis, told her and Agent Chan to back off Kenny Lake, Audra Solis took matters into her own hands. She and Agent Chan staked out at his house or Sunshine's apartment, getting pictures of him, watching his every move and interactions with the Montoyas. Once she felt she had enough leverage, she processed the next part of her plan. She waited until Kenny went to work at the police station, then both she and Agent Chan went to their door and knocked on it.

Aida opened the door and was going to close it until Audra showed her black and white stills of Kenny and Sunshine making love and shopping for baby clothes. She let them into the living room to talk, but in the end, Aida was a dead end. Even as emotionally crushed as she was, she could do the investigation no good. Audra still had one more play, and she hoped it would work out for her.

Rodamez invited Kenny to his mansion to discuss business. While he was there, he noticed a work crew installing a large electronic safe in the main study; then when the crew was done with the installment, they cleared out, leaving Rodamez the seven-digit safe combination.

"Max, help me load this money into the safe," Rodamez said, pointing to four bags on the floor. Both men loaded the duffel bags into the safe. When they were finished, Rodamez punched in the seven-digit code, locking the safe. Kenny snuck a peak over his shoulder and punched the seven numbers into his cell phone under the name Cartel Umberto.

"So what's the business you need me to do?" Kenny asked, reclining in a beach chair next to Rodamez on the Montoya mansion poolside.

Rodamez looked over at him. "I got this deal going down for fifty kilos, and I need both you and Cody there for support," he said.

"I don't have a problem with it, but that might not be such a good idea to bring Cody along," he said.

"Why not, Max, I thought Cody was your boy?" Rodamez said, full of questions.

Kenny nodded. "Was, but I've caught him stealing from us both. The kilos that were coming up missing were all him. I caught him in the act stealing out of the club and confronted him about it. That's when we had the fight. The reason I am telling you this is because he told me he wants out. He says he was only loyal to Umberto. Now that he is gone, it's no telling what he'll do," Kenny said, shrugging his shoulders.

"So what do you say, Max, are you in or out of this transaction with the kilos?" Rodamez asked.

"Yeah, I'm in, but what about Cody?" Kenny said.

"Don't worry about Cody. I'll take care of anybody that steals from me," he said.

Kenny started to like Rodamez Montoya more than he thought he would. Too bad he would have to set him up to take a fall and steal all his money. "So who are we meeting with?" Kenny asked.

"A few guys from the Crip gang, they finally broke down and came crawling on their hands and knees to us. They're lucky I don't exterminate them all. I am not the face of peace my brother was," he said.

"I see." Kenny nodded his head in agreement.

"I'm going to Mexico in a few days. While I'm gone, I need you to look over the shipping operation and the club. I'll be back in a week," he said.

"No problem. You know I got you," Kenny said.

"Good," Rodamez said.

Kenny felt good as he strolled into the living room of his home with Aida. All he could think of was that he was the acting don of the Montoya Cartel. Yes, him, an undercover servant of the peace. He was truly proud of himself.

He flopped down on his couch to take a load off. Aida walked into the living room with a stack of papers in her hand. She walked over to Kenny and slapped him across the face with the papers.

"What the fuck, Aida?" he screamed.

"Look at the pictures, Kenny. They don't lie," she said, tossing him the pictures the IA had given her of the affair he was having with Sunshine.

"Where did you get this bullshit?" Kenny said, looking at the black-and-white stills.

"The IA, Kenny! I want you out. I want a divorce," she said, tears welling up in her eyes and spilling over.

"Wait, baby, holdup. It ain't like that," Kenny said.

"Kenny, just go. I already talked to Sunshine. I know she is pregnant. Just go to your whore. I can't deal with this or you right now. You sleeping on the couch just won't work tonight," she said.

Kenny pulled his black Range Rover into Sunshine's apartment parking lot just as Agents Audra Solis and Peter Chan were leaving. He missed them by a millisecond. He went into the apartment and got straight into bed. He needed to think. He thought the IA had gotten off his back, but they hadn't, so he knew sooner or later, he would end up in jail if he stayed in Sunset. He needed to get out of the United States, period, but he didn't have enough money to just uproot and live life well off. He knew where he could get it first thing in the morning. He will meet with John and put a plan together.

Darryl Johnson woke up and took a shower, then he got dressed. He couldn't stop thinking about his meeting with the Internal Affairs director and how he just shut down everything. He told him about Kenny, John, and Sergeant Steven Dooner; then he was worried about the fact he had not seen or heard from Nicole Brown in almost a week. He had a feeling Kenny had something to do with her disappearance.

Darryl had made up his mind—he was going to blow the whistle on the whole operation. He was scheduled to meet with Agent Audra Solis within the hour. Darryl walked out of his house and got into his black 2000 Chevy Monte Carlo. He stuck his key into the ignition and turned it. The engine clicked, but instead of turning over, the car bomb attached to the gas tank ignited, blowing the car up.

9

A MASTER PLAN

"I'm telling you, John, I have the code to the safe. It's like about four million in there. I helped put it in there. It's easy money, and we are set for life," Kenny said.

"Then why don't we just go get the money right now while he's out of town?" John asked.

"Because Rodamez wants me to meet with him and the Sunset NHCs for a deal of fifty kilos. Figure we can get that money also and split," he said, picking up his hamburger and taking a bite.

"I don't know, K, that might be a little too greedy and cost us," John said, looking around the restaurant as though someone were monitoring their conversation.

"Man, J, it's easy. We stick up the Sunset Crips and the Montoyas, then we roll back to the Montoyas, split the safe, and get ghost out of the States," Kenny said with surety.

"What about Darryl and Steven?" John asked.

"Man, fuck Darryl and John. Besides you and me, ain't nobody down for this shit," Kenny said.

"I don't know, Ken, maybe we can get Gomez and Sanchez," John said, taking a handful of french fries and shoving them into his mouth.

"All right, Johnny baby, if you can get them, cool. If not, we move solo at the end of the week," Kenny said.

When the two men finished eating their meals, they left the restaurant and went their separate ways.

"So, Kenny, are you going to marry me, or what?" Sunshine asked, laying next to Kenny the next morning.

"Sunshine, don't be crazy. You know I'm never going to leave my wife. I'm only here every day 'cause she kicked me out. You know I love her, stop trippin'," he said, getting out of the bed to go take a shower.

When Sunshine heard the water running, she picked up the phone on the nightstand. She dug into her purse, pulling out a white business card. She dialed the number and listened to it ring until a female with a country accent answered it.

"Hello, this is Sunshine, Kenny's girlfriend. If you still want my help, just tell me. I'll do whatever you need, Ms. Solis."

Kenny, John, and Detectives Sanches and Gomez met in the vacant warehouse where the meeting between the Montoya cartel and the SS NHC members would meet to have the drug transaction.

"It's simple, man, we are going to come in here. I'm going to be with the Montoyas. Ya'll hide behind these old crates. When the drugs and money come out, ya'll three come out and get everything. The four of us will just walk out of here and go to the parking garage, load it into my Range Rover, and roll. It's simple—we make the split, and within an hour, we're all right, men. Ricky, you can take out ya boy Danny's wife, and, Tamino, you can go get that bypass—uh—gastric surgery you want," Kenny said, making light of a real situation.

All the men started to laugh. "So you two in, or what?" John asked.

"I'm in," Ricky said.

"How about you, Tamino?" Kenny asked.

"Yeah, I'm in, hold on a second," he said, answering the phone ringing in his pocket. "Hello? Huh? What? You don't say? I'm partnered up with Gomez today. Yeah, sure, we'll be right there," he said into the phone.

"What's that all about?" Ricky asked his partner.

"That was Danny. He said he wants us to come to a crime scene across town. Somebody just took out Darryl at his house with a car bomb. We gotta go. We'll see ya'll there. Come on Rick," he said. The two men got up and left the warehouse.

"Your doing?" John asked Kenny with a skeptical look.

"Naw, Rodamez. He needed to go, though, he was getting too sloppy," Kenny said matter-of-factly.

"Are you going to the scene?" he asked. Kenny shook his head.

"Man, fuck work and Darryl, I'm a free agent now," he said.

At the end of the week, Kenny walked into the warehouse with Rodamez and four of his men, all armed with AK-47s. The six Sunset Neighborhood Crips were already there with Uzis, MAC-11s, and TEC-9s. John, Tamino, and Ricky were hidden out of sight armed with the MAC-10 they had taken from Yo Yo Jenkins and the AK-47. John held two stolen .45 Glock pistols with extra clips. All three men wore bulletproof vest.

Agents Audra Solis and Peter Chan followed Kenny from Sunshine's apartment to Club Destiny and, from there, to the vacant warehouse on Sentry Lane. They sat and waited for him to come out of the warehouse. Once he did, they would make their arrest with or without a search warrant. They already had enough evidence to hold him.

Once the meeting got underway, Kenny noticed one of the gang members kept eyeing him. He found himself trying to remember the hood's face, but he couldn't. The man studied him head to toe, trying to do the same. It came to them both around the same time. Just as their faces registered, both men knew they were in trouble. No drugs or money had been brought out, and things were going to shit.

"Damn."

"Awe, cuzz! That nigga right there is the police. These niggas' is five-0!" BadLuck screamed, pointing to Kenny and the Montoya men.

"What? No. What the fuck is he talking about?" Rodamez said, trying to make sense of what he was hearing.

Kenny aimed the AK-47 at BadLuck and squeezed off six quick rounds that blew through the gang member's chest and abdomen, igniting the war.

Bullets flew from both sides as they scrambled for cover. John and Ricky came from behind two big crates on the right side of the warehouse, guns blazing. They cut down two of the Montoya men. Outside of the warehouse, Audra and Peter could hear the thunderous explosions of some machine guns and assault rifles. Audra turned to

Peter and nodded. Both the IA agents got out of the car and pulled their government-issue 9 mm Sig Sauer and headed for the warehouse.

Audra led into the war zone gun first. She saw Tamino firing a MAC-10 wildly at two men hiding behind a big copper pipe.

"Freeze and drop your weapon, Detective!" Peter called out.

Tamino turned around and faced the IA agents, sending a hail of bullets at them from the sputtering submachine gun.

Audra ducked behind an iron steam pipe while Peter dropped down to one knee and squeezed off one round from the Sig, which took Tamino Sanches between the eyes, snapping his head back on his neck and sending his limp body crashing to the floor.

Rodamez Montoya didn't know what was what and who was on his side and who wasn't. Now his only concern was survival. He sprung up from behind the wooden crate he hid had behind for cover and, down on one knee, took aim at the IA agent with his .50 Desert Eagle. He squeezed the big hand cannon's trigger, blasting four hollow-tipped rounds into and through Peter Chan's vest and into his chest, killing him instantly. Audra saw the bullets fly through her partner's chest then watched his lifeless body crumble to the ground. She took aim on Rodamez, but he went for cover before she could take her shot.

She kneeled next to her fallen comrade and put her index and middle finger to his neck. There was no pulse. She stood up and crept through the warehouse again. She saw Ricky Gomez pinned down by two of the Sunset gang members. Agent Audra Solis aimed with her Sig and pulled the trigger three times. The kick from the gun jerked in her hands, but her aim rang true. She hit Ricky Gomez in the face. The bullet entered his right eye and tore up into his brain. Her other two bullets hit both of the Crips in the forehead, flipping them backward into the crates behind them. Another man opened up on her with a TEC-9. She dove to the ground for cover.

Kenny jumped up from his cover and ran for the front of the warehouse. Carlos and Rodamez followed behind him. John saw Santino try to run for the door and emptied two magazines in his back. He reloaded his empty pistols and came out of his cover with both guns blazing at the three remaining Crips. He cut down the man that had Audra Solis pinned down on the ground first; then he spun his murderous makers of death on the other two street hoods, looked them both in the eyes, and blew them away. John holstered his guns and walked out of the warehouse through the back of a loading dock.

Kenny came running top speed out of the old Springdale warehouse. He could still hear the gunfire from the inside. He heard automatic rifle reports again, but this time, he could hear bullets whizzing by his ears. He dove for cover behind a wooden crate some ways from the warehouse's front door. He gripped the .45 in his hand and tried to shoot over the crate, but the gun's slide just came open. It was empty. He ejected the empty magazine, letting it fall to the ground. Then he dug into his back pocket and pulled out a full clip. He rammed the magazine into the gun, but there was more gunfire in the warehouse.

Rodamez and Carlos came running through the front door; Kenny came up from his cover with the reloaded .45 and popped off four shots at the unsuspecting men. The first bullet hit Santino in the neck; the other two bullets slammed into his chest, lifting him off his feet, sending him flying into a glass window and back into the warehouse. The fourth round went whizzing by Rodamez and skinned his neck. Kenny locked eyes with Rodamez, who he raised the Desert Eagle. Kenny knew he was outgunned and dove back behind his cover just as the bullets came flying out of Rodamez's gun and tore into the crate, splitting the wooden box. Fragments of wood flew into Kenny's eyes and face. He felt blood running down the side of his head from a cut over his left eyebrow.

"Max, show yourself. You come out now, Max! We need to talk!" Rodamez screamed with a thick accent.

Kenny knew he had to get out of there before Rodamez opened up with the Desert Eagle again.

"Hey, Max, you greedy muthafucka. You fucked me! What did I tell you, son of a bitch, you fuck me and you're dead! You're dead, muthafucka!" he screamed.

Kenny thought hard about his next move. He tightened his grip on the butt of the .45 again; he shoved the gun over the splintered crate and took four shots without looking. Rodamez dove for cover after Kenny laid down his cover shots. Kenny jumped to his feet and sprinted to the Springdale warehouse parking garage. Rodamez reloaded his pistol and chased after Kenny. Kenny ran top speed into the garage, searching for his truck. His experience as a track star in high school paid off for him, giving him a huge distance between himself and Rodamez.

Kenny found his truck parked backward in two compact parking stalls. Kenny stuck his left hand in his pocket and fished out the keys to the black Range Rover. He pushed the disarm button, unlocking the truck doors. Kenny opened the door and slid into the driver seat. He closed the door and set the .45 on the dashboard. He slid the truck key into the ignition and started up the Range Rover. As he threw the truck in gear and drove out of the parking garage, Rodamez stepped in front of the truck, taking aim at him. Kenny ducked his head behind the steering wheel as Rodamez pumped the front of the truck full of bullets, shooting into the truck's engine lights and grill. Kenny gunned the wounded motor, sending the truck straight at the shooting Montoya.

Realizing the truck was headed straight for him, Rodamez tried to jump out the way at the last minute, but he didn't move fast enough, and the big truck clipped his left leg, snapping the bones. Rodamez hit the ground on his right side, aiming the gun at the side of the truck, squeezing off the last few rounds in the Desert Eagle's magazine. Kenny drove out onto the street.

After John McBeth stopped shooting and walked out of the warehouse, Audra pushed up from the ground with her pistol in hand. She ran out the front of the warehouse, passing the corpse of Carlos on the broken glass and wood he landed on. Audra ran into the warehouse parking garage when she arrived she found Rodamez Montoya on the ground holding the empty Desert Eagle.

"Montoya, put the gun down!" Audra demanded.

"Fuck you, bitch," he said, pointing the gun at her.

Audra did not hesitate and squeezed off one quick round, which hit the wounded man in the forehead between the eyes. She stepped over Rodamez's body and spit on him. "That was for Peter, you bastard," she said, pulling out her cell phone and calling the local police.

Afterward, she called Sunshine. She made sure she left the warehouse before any law enforcement arrived. She could not afford to be held up with questioning. There was a killer out there on the loose that she intended to stop on her own.

Once he was clear of the shooting death trap at the Springdale warehouse, Kenny allowed his mind to take in what had just transpired between him and his fallen comrades, Ricky and Tamino, and he had no idea if John even made it out. He knew robbing Rodamez was dangerous as hell, but he had him right where he needed, and BadLuck had to mess up everything. He should have took him down during the raids. Now he was out of the fifty kilos, $675,000, and three friends.

"Damn!" he shouted, slamming his foot down on the gas pedal, putting more distance between himself and the Springdale warehouse massacre.

When Kenny made it across town, he pulled the big and battered SUV to a stop inside a big grocery store parking lot. The truck itself was a mess, and even Kenny was amazed at how far he had come in the truck without it stalling on him.

"Aaah shit!" Kenny screamed as he tried to step out of the truck. He looked down at his leg and saw the flesh on his right thigh had been ripped open, probably from a bullet Rodamez had sent flying into the truck. He needed stitches for sure to close the gaping gash in his leg, but he did not have the time.

He climbed back into the truck and closed the door; he reached over to the glove box and pulled out a container of baby wipes, a handful of restaurant napkins, and a roll of duct tape. Kenny went to work cleaning and stuffing napkins down into the open wound. Once it was no longer bleeding, Kenny made a field dressing out of the napkins and taped them in place with the strong duct tape. Kenny leaned back in the driver's seat and grabbed the .45 off the dashboard and focused on the automatic doors of Tom's grocery store, searching for his next victim. He planned on carjacking the first person he saw by themselves.

As Kenny waited, he noticed a black-and-white police cruiser pulling over a drunk driver in a blue 1996 Pontiac and telling the driver to stay put. With the .45 in hand, Kenny lay down in the driver's seat of the truck as though he were dead. The officer removed his side arm and crept over to the driver side.

"Sir, are you all right?" he asked, looking through the window at Kenny.

"Help me, help," Kenny whispered.

"Oh my god," the officer said, returning the gun to its holster in order to help the injured man. When he secured his weapon, he looked back into the truck. Kenny unloaded two rounds into the officer's face, killing him on contact. Kenny stepped out of the truck into the rapidly pooling blood of the executed officer. He walked over to the now stunned driver, who just witnessed the execution. Kenny opened the Firebird door and yanked the drunken woman out by her shirt collar. He got into the car and tossed her purse. She just looked at the large black man starting up the car.

"At least you didn't get a ticket," he said, laughing as he drove off to Rodamez's mansion.

10

THE END GAME

Kenny pulled to a stop next to the Pontiac in front of Rodamez's mansion. He got out and was welcomed by the guards who all looked at his bloody right pant leg.

"What's going on, Max? What happened to your leg?" one of the guards asked, then he pointed to Kenny's eyebrow. "And your face?"

"Believe it or not, I fell through a glass window at home. I was moving too fast, didn't know my patio door was closed, busted straight through it. It's not as bad as it looks. I'm headed to the doctor after I make this drop for the boss," Kenny said, spinning a believable tale.

Kenny walked into Rodamez's study. He closed the door and pulled his cell phone out of his pocket. He brought the code for the safe up on the screen. Kenny punched the seven digits into the safe keypad and twisted the handle. The safe came open, and Kenny saw two duffel bags filled with money. He zipped both of the bags closed and lifted them over his shoulders. He should have done what John suggested in the first place and just hit the safe and got on, but his greed caused everybody to get hurt.

Kenny walked out of the mansion, leaving the safe and study open. He walked by all the Montoya guards with a smile on his face and both bags. He loaded the duffel bags into the back seat of the Pontiac. He got into the car and drove out of Rodamez Montoya's mansion.

This was easy over all, he thought, looking at the bags in the back seat. He pulled his cell phone out of his pants pocket and called Sunshine as he drove. "Sunshine, it's me. Don't talk, just listen. Write down this address. When you get ready, let me know," he said.

"I'm good," she said, grabbing an ink pen and a piece of paper.

"11600 West Wall Street, public storage number 16. I'm going to drop off two bags of money there. Within thirty minutes, I want you to go pick up the money. I'm going to leave the key on the back tire of the blue Pontiac Firebird parked out on the street. I want you to get the money and take a cruise to Cuba, from Cuba, you'll head to Fiji where I'll be waiting for you. I'll call you when I'm headed to the airport, baby. I love you," he said.

"I love you too," she said, hanging up the phone.

"Was that him?" Audra Solis asked, sitting on Sunshine's couch.

"No it was my aunt, giving me a cooking recipe I asked for—jerk chicken. Don't worry, he'll call, and you'll be able to nail his date-rapin' ass," she said, more upset with Kenny wanting another woman than him actually raping her.

Kenny pulled into the public storage and parked on the street. He walked down the lot with the two big bags to his storage space. He opened the rolling garage and put the two bags down. He redressed his leg, then he went through the few clothes he kept in the storage. He got dressed in a blue Derek Jeter baseball jersey and a pair of blue sweatpants and a pair of white Jumpmans. Kenny closed the box his clothes and shoes came out of. He picked up a sock and wiped down the .45 to clean off his fingerprints. He put on a pair of latex gloves, tucked the gun down the back of his pants, and closed the garage door.

He walked out to the Firebird parked on the curb and put the storage key on the back tire. He took the cell phone out of his pocket and called Sunshine again. "Aye, baby, I'm going to the airport now. I got the bags in the back of the storage under a blanket. I'll call you when I take off. Make sure you are not followed. Shit, got kind of bad today, that's why I can't come there," he said.

"Where are you going, Kenny, what is all this about?" she asked.

"I'm flying to Columbia. I can't get into everything right now. I'll call later. I gotta call me a cab," Kenny said.

Kenny hung up the phone and called a cab to pick him up. Kenny arrived at the airport and went straight to the counter to buy a ticket to Columbia. He waited in the lobby until his flight. Kenny felt exhausted and dozed off in his chair.

"That was him. He's headed to the airport and getting a flight to Columbia," Sunshine told the vigilante Internal Affairs agent.

"Is that all?" Audra asked her.

"Yeah, that's it," she answered.

"Good. Thank you for your help, Sunshine. I want you to stay here where you will be safe I'm going to get this bastard," she said.

"I'll be here. You be careful," Sunshine said, showing Audra out of the apartment.

By this time tomorrow, I'll be a millionaire with my wife. I'll send for Sunshine to stay later. Yeah, that's it. After she gives me my score, I'll send her back home, Kenny thought, coming out of a dream. He checked his watch. His flight departure was fast approaching. He grabbed his cell phone off his lap and called his wife.

"Baby, it's me—no, don't hang up. Look, listen, I came up today. We are set up for life. Everything you want, you can have—we can have. Do you hear me?" he asked.

"I hear you, Kenny, but I don't have time. You're a cheater. I'm sure Sunshine would love to spend the perfect life with you because I don't want to," she said dismissively.

"Flight one eighty seven is now boarding at gate two twelve" came over the airport loudspeaker. Kenny stood up and picked his passport off the seat next to him. He pressed the cell phone to his ear as he walked through the lobby, oblivious of everything around him.

"Look, Aida, don't do this baby. I'm going to Columbia. I want you to come out tomorrow. We can start all over, baby," he said.

"Detective Lake, put the phone down and put your hands up. You are under arrest," Audra said from behind his back with her Sig aimed at his spine.

"Fuck, baby, I gotta go," he said, turning around to face Audra and the 9 mm she now turned on his chest.

"Kenny, what's going on? What's the matter?" Aida screamed into the phone. Kenny closed the phone, cutting off the connection with his wife. He went to his waist to clip his phone onto his pants.

Audra knew Kenny was putting away his phone, but she pulled the trigger of her gun anyway, sending a bullet flying through Kenny's chest on the right side. The bullet tore through Kenny's lung and shoulder bone and lodged in his clavicle.

Kenny felt a burst of instant pain in his chest. He dropped his phone and passport to the floor and felt for the gaping hole in his chest. He fell back to the floor, his whole body ablaze, then he went numb, his body twitching. Blood started to pour out of his mouth. He could see people running around all over the airport in panic. The last thing he saw were paramedics tending to him. An oxygen mask was put over his mouth as he closed his eyes.

Sunshine did not intend to ever go to Columbia, Cuba, or Fiji with Kenny once he had said he wouldn't be with her. She turned him to the IA. When Audra left her apartment, she got in the Nissan Z Kenny had bought her and headed over to the public storage. She saw the Firebird out on the street and got the key off the back tire and opened storage 16. She went inside the space and pulled the cover off the two duffel bags. She hit the dirt when she looked at the money. She took the money, over four million in cash, and flew by private jet to Costa Rica, where she planned on spending the rest of her life with her son, who was growing inside her.

Detective John McBeth walked out of the Springdale warehouse, went to his house, and cleared out his safe, taking all his illegal monies. Then he went to his bank and cleared out his checking and saving accounts. John drove his truck across town to a small airport, got into an airplane, and disappeared, leaving it all behind—his wife, his kids, his job, his home, his whole life.

Agent Audra Solis was put under investigation for the unnecessary use of force, shooting down an unarmed man through the chest in an airport full of people. Audra was looked upon as a villain shooting an undercover detective until the investigation against her was dropped Audra became a local hero, the face of justice, and received high praise from taking down a whole corrupt police department. She received a promotion as the supervisor of Internal Affairs.

James Willis was sentenced to two years in federal prison for tampering with evidence and obstruction of justice. Audra went and got counseling and established a problem for rape victims Audra Solis reformed the Internal Affairs. The Sunset chief of police, Thomas O'Brien, resigned from his position out of shame from his lack of control and justice of his detectives. Danny Zamora and Jenny Hall were both transferred to a new police department's beat division. When Ricky Gomez was murdered at the Springdale warehouse shooting, Danny's wife, Claudia, Ricky's lover, committed suicide. Danny would never recover and quit the force and, soon after, became a homeless drunk.

Officer Jenny hall could not stand her new assignment. Her pay was reduced, and she was not comfortable in her own skin. It was why she worked undercover in the first place. She also quit the force and went to work at the strip club. She liked the attention she got as a dancer in Club Destiny, and the pay was better, so she took the stage full time.

Sergeant Steven Dooner found the front door of his Pacific beach house broken and a task force stormed in to arrest him on numerous charges of murder, attempted murder, conspiracy to commit murder, and conspiracy to commit robbery. The sergeant was convicted on all counts, even for the murders of Detectives Sam Garboski and Darryl Johnson, in which case he had no direct connection to. Before it was all said and done, James Willis testified on behalf of the state that Steven put him up to getting the Internal Affairs off his corrupt detectives. The sergeant was also given an obstruction of justice charge at his sentencing. Steven Dooner was sentenced to death by lethal injection.

After Kenny Lake was shot down almost to death in the airport by Audra Solis, he was rushed to the Sunset Mercy ER, where the doctors were able to remove the bullet from his chest without nerve damage. After the surgery, Kenny was sent off to the Sunset County Jail to await his arraignment. Kenny was charged with several murders, obstruction of justice, robbery, and various conspiracies. Kenny took the first deal the state offered him. Kenny had only taken the deal to stay out of death row. He already saw what happened to Steven Dooner. Kenny wasn't going to sit on anybody's death row; instead, he was given 511 years to life in prison until Audra filed rape charges, so Kenny took a five-year deal for that, leaving him in Sunset Lasey Prison with 516 years to life without the possibility of parole.

At Sunset Lasey, Kenny did all his time main line. He refused to go into protective custody, so he walked the yard ex-cop with the rest of the convicts. His time seemed to fly by in the small cell. He spent most of his time reading and writing. He completed two books, one autobiography and another on how to catch a crooked cop.

Sunshine sent him several postcards and on occasion a letter here or there. She was out in Costa Rica, spending his millions raising his son. Kenny was furious. He was wrong about Sunshine. She was nothing like his mother. Kenny wanted to ring her neck for being so greedy.

On Kenny's thirty-third birthday, he stepped out of his cell on the third tier for the morning breakfast movement when he saw a light-skinned man with a long black ponytail break formation and come toward him at a rapid pace. Kenny's focus was locked on the man's face, trying to identify the approaching hulk of a man. His attention was so consumed with identifying who the man was he became vulnerable to the sharpened piece of jagged steel in the man's hand. By the time Kenny recognized who the man was, it was too late.

Cyco jabbed the sharp, jagged makeshift knife into his chest, side, and stomach and pushed Kenny over the railing of the tier, sending him crashing three stories down to the prison floor. The Sunset Neighborhood Crip had done three years for Kenny ratting on him, and now they were even.

Aida Lake did the only thing she knew how to do in life. She stayed loyal to her husband. She brought everything Kenny needed. She also moved closer to the prison so she could visit Kenny every weekend.

I hate it here. Maybe I should kill myself when I get out of this body cast, Kenny thought as he lay in bed while Aida spoon-fed him ice cream during an infirmary visit. He could not bear spending the rest of his life in prison.

THE BLOWER
ROMEO CONWAY

PART 1

The dark-skinned Columbian man sat comfortably in his favorite Italian leather recliner. He held his favorite weapon, wiping it down with a cotton cloth, immersed by the unique pistol. He looked down at the shiny chrome .45 semiautomatic with a focused, concentrated look on his face. His dark-brown eyes were glossy and distant, almost as though he were in a trance. To an observer, one would think he was cleaning and oiling a regular gun, but the gun Titto Perez held in his hands was far from the norm. Nope, this was no ordinary piece.

Titto's thoughts raced back in time three years ago when he first laid eyes on the gun. He was still fairly new to the United States, and he didn't feel safe out in the crime-infested Miami streets. Titto contacted another Columbian immigrant he had known from across the sea. The two men had come up from the dangerous streets of one of Columbia's fiercest ghettos. They were good friends then and remained good friends stateside. When Titto met with his friend, Castor Sato, the men embraced each other. Sato patted Titto on the back and smiled as they broke their embrace.

"You made it, Titto, what took you so long?" Sato asked as the two men stood in front of a hot dog stand.

Titto looked up and down the busy street. "I never wanted to come here," Titto said, pointing at the flashy cars as they zoomed by on the main boulevard. "I got in a lot of trouble, killed a few bad men, so I had to get on a boat and come here," he said with his broken English accent.

"I understand," Sato said, nodding his head. "I got a job in my business for you. I make thousands out here, and I need a bodyguard, an enforcer," he added, hoping his friend would accept his offer. He knew better than anyone else how skilled in the art of murder Titto was.

"Sure, Castor, I'll help you out, but I need a gun, a big gun," Titto said.

Castor Sato took Titto to a small Jamaican pawnshop in Dade. The shop was a green-stuccoed hole in the wall with a big window facing the street. There was a display in the front of what looked like a real headless chicken with blood running out of its neck onto its body. Above was a red-and-green sign with neon lights that read Joo Joo's Pawn and Voodoo Shop. Titto looked at the shop then looked over at Sato, who tapped him on the shoulder. "It's the right place," he said, reading Titto's mind.

They walked inside the shop and went straight to the store counter. There was a small black man wearing a black T-shirt with a marijuana leaf printed on the front. The man was almost as black as the shirt he wore. His long black-and-gold dreadlocks draped over his shoulders under a red, black, yellow, and green knitted skully.

The man stared at the two Columbian men as they walked into the shop. "What can I do you fo', mon?" he asked as they stepped up to the counter.

Sato looked at the Rasta then to the glass counter laced with various handguns of all calibers and sizes. "We need a gun for my friend here," Sato said, pointing at Titto.

The Jamaican man smiled, revealing a mouth full of rotten teeth. "Got just ta ting for ya, mon," he said, sliding open the glass case. He reached in and pulled out a chrome .380 with a pearl handle. He handed the unloaded gun to Titto, who was busy looking at other weapons in the glass display case.

Titto grabbed the gun, held it with both hands, and squeezed the trigger. "No, bigger!" he shouted, handing the gun back to the Jamaican, refocusing his attention on the case.

The Jamaican put the .380 back into the glass case and removed a black .357 revolver and a blue steel Colt Python. "Here is bigga fo' ya, mon." The Jamaican slid the two guns across the counter toward Titto. The shopkeeper's words seem to fall upon deaf ears because neither Sato nor Titto responded.

Titto found himself transfixed on the weapons in the case while Sato found himself fixated on the expression on Titto's face as he studied one gun in particular in the case. Titto felt as though he was being drawn into some form of spell by the gun in the glass case. There were twenty guns or more in that case, yet this one chrome .45 seemed to shine bright like a diamond in the rough.

"Titto, Titto!" the gun called him. "Don't you want me?"

"Titto, Titto!" he heard a familiar voice snap him out of his trance. "Titto, do you want these?" Sato asked, pointing to the two guns the Jamaican had on the counter.

"No, this," Titto said, pointing to the chrome .45 in the case.

"Ah!" the Jamaican man grunted, shaking his head from side to side, and dropped the two pistols back into the display case. "No, no, no, mon," he said, waving his index finger back and forth. "It's cursed, mon, it got voodoo on it," he warned.

"I want this gun," Titto said sternly.

"No, mon, dis gun be cursed. Got mind of its own. Its tell of white devil kill Jamaican family, so famous witch doctor put a black magic curse on him, banish devil soul to gun forever, mon!" the Jamaican said.

"Hocus pocus? Just give him the gun, maine," Sato mocked.

"No! Me won' touch it, mon, me won' even put it in de case, mon. Don't touch it. It consume you, mon, possess you. It enslave you, mon," he warned again.

Titto heard nothing that the shop owner said. He wanted that .45. "I want it!" he shouted.

"You want it? You get it yourself, mon," the Jamaican said as he stepped back from the counter, shaking his head.

"I'll get it myself," Titto said, reaching over the counter, leaning on the glass case and putting his hand over the handle of the .45. The pistol seemed to vibrate in his palm. Titto pulled the gun back over the counter and cocked back the slide, revealing an empty chamber.

Sato pulled a thick wad of cash from his pocket. He counted off ten hundred-dollar bills and handed them to the Jamaican man. Titto aimed the unloaded gun at the Jamaican man and squeezed the trigger. The gun clicked sharply when the hammer fell on the empty chamber, forcing the slide back. The Jamaican man flinched when the slide racked backward, revealing the nose of the .45 barrel.

"You go ta hell with that devil pistol. You gon' regret it, mon! You gon' regret it!" he screamed after Titto and Sato, stuffing the crisp Benjamins in his pockets as they walked out of the shop.

Titto worked nonstop for his best friend. Several hits were ordered on behalf of Sato's port of Miami, Columbian Mafia. The first murder Titto committed was still fresh in his memory. Every so often, he would suddenly smell the mixture of gunpowder and blood as though it just happened ten minutes ago. There was another Columbian, an older immigrant named Pablo Salazar, trying to smuggle cocaine into the States through Sato's turf. Salazar was told to either take another route or take a dirt nap. Not one to be frightened by threats, Salazar spit in the face of the Sato messenger. Titto found himself dispatched to a nightclub in Daytona. He carried the chrome .45 with an extended clip in a holster at the small of his back. On the pistol's service end was affixed a hinch husher. He concealed the weapon with a basic blue-and-white flower button-up shirt over blue jeans and sandals without socks. To the average man or woman, he appeared to be a regular club-goer, but he wasn't. He was an assassin who walked right up to Pablo Salazar's table, pulled the glowing .45 from the small of his back, and squeezed the trigger at point-blank range. The gun sputtered six times in his hand before he took his finger off the trigger. Salazar tried to rise from the table after seeing Titto pull his pistol, but he was too late. The six rounds went into Salazar's chest and throat, killing him instantly.

Titto looked down at the gun in his hand. He squeezed the trigger once and got full fire. *What had just happened?* he wondered. "I told ja, mon, it's cursed," the Jamaican shopkeeper's voice ripped through his consciousness.

When Titto snapped back into his zone of killing, he wiped the splatters of blood from his face with the back of his hand. There was screams coming from all over the club as people scattered to find the exit. The shock of the gun almost kept him from finishing his mission. Pablo Salazar's dinner companion tried to get up and run for an exit herself. Titto took aim and squeezed the trigger, sending eight more rapid burst of hot lead flying out of the .45. The bullets cut into the woman's neck, severing her spinal cord from her skull and tearing into her back.

"Fuck," Titto said. He could not believe what had just happened. He looked at the gun in his hand before putting it back into its holster and walking out of the nightclub.

Titto tried to tell his good friend about the shooting at the nightclub and the .45. Sato didn't pay Titto much attention. Instead, he just handed him more contracts of people he wanted eliminated. After a while, Titto had done so many hits he was promoted to kingpin. As Sato's second in command, he sat comfortably on top of the drug world. Titto was satisfied where he was and with what he had, but every time, he held his gun, he wanted more.

"White devil neva satisfied, mon, te greedy mon," Titto envisioned the Jamaican man saying.

Titto had a nice house, a Porsche, a Benz, and a Jag from his position as the number 2 man—nothing in the world was outside of his reach. Even still, as he held the .45, he felt unappreciated and underpaid. The gun seemed to glow in his hand, fueling his newfound passion and obsession for more.

When Titto confronted his good friend Castor Sato at his Miami fortress, they had a few drinks as they discussed business, and Titto mentioned how he felt. "I should become partner instead of a regular member of the organization," he said.

Sato looked at him confused. He sat behind his large oak desk, scratching his head. He could not believe what he was hearing because he himself had never viewed himself as a man who didn't provide his men with all they needed, especially Titto. Sato had given Titto everything, even when he didn't understand what he was getting or deserve what he had given him. Sato felt betrayed that Titto would even make such a request, after all he had done for him. He looked at Titto from across his desk. He did not recognize the man before him. He had never noticed and never saw the signs, but Titto's appearance gave it away.

Titto was using. Why else would he be making such an unworthy request? Sato looked at Titto and noticed his eyes were sunken into the eye sockets of his skull. He had not shaved in what seemed to be about a month. His suit looked wrinkled and dirty, his hair was oily and wild looking, as if he had not kept it up. His hands and fingertips looked bruised and raw, with a thin oily film on them. This was not the friend Sato had grown up with in the Columbia ghetto playing *futbol*. No, the man before him was a shell of his friend.

"Titto, maybe you ought to take a vacation or something. You don't look too good. Have you been getting any sleep?" he asked, noticing the heavy black bags under Titto's eyes.

"What?" he asked taken aback by the question. "I asked you for a partnership and you tell me to take a fuckin' vacation?"

"Calm down, Titto. Are you using?" Sato asked.

"No. I'm not sleeping, maine, but I ain't usin' no dope, maine," Titto said in his heavy Columbian accent. He was angered by the question.

"You look like shit," Sato said, rising from his seat behind his desk.

Titto was tired. His eyes were heavy, and he could barely stay awake lately because of his sleepless nights. Titto would sit wide awake every night oiling and cleaning the gun. He even began speaking to the pistol. Sometimes he thought he heard the gun speak back, and when it did, it said "Take control" or "You deserve more" or "You are the real boss, kill him!" Titto had no intentions of killing his best friend, but now with his bouts of anger and lack of sleep, the gun was commanding him to act strangely.

"Aye, maine, maybe you oughta go sleep off whatever you goin' through, maine," Sato said, walking around the desk and putting his hand on his good friend's shoulder.

Titto's body seemed to move without his command. He quickly rose from the leather chair he had sat in, reached into his disheveled suit jacket, and put his sore hand onto the butt of the .45. His hand seemed to fit like a glove around the gun handle. Titto's eyes lit up when he freed the gun from its big leather casing.

Sato stood at Titto's side in disbelief, frozen. He could not believe his best friend would pull a gun on him. Still, he never thought Titto would ever use it on him. Titto himself thought the same thing as he turned to Sato, looked him in the eyes, aimed the pistol, and squeezed the trigger. The bullets jumped out of the gun with ease. The first spray of bullets hit Castor in the face, shattering his cranium and cutting through his brain like a Ginsu knife cutting through sushi. Blood, brains, and pieces of his splintered skull splattered on Titto's clothes and face as Sato's lifeless body fell hard to the ground, knocking his deck chair over. A guard kicked in the front door of Sato's office when he heard the crashing sound. He stepped into the room and aimed his Uzi at Titto. Titto spun around quickly and squeezed the .45 trigger, sending a wave of bullets into the guard's upper torso. The guard slumped against the office door, eyes wide open and dead, just like his boss Castor Sato.

After Titto murdered Sato, he used the men loyal to him in the cartel to get established as the new head of the Columbian Mafia. Three years later, he was the king of Florida's drug market, and he owed it all to the .45 Sato bought him at the small Jamaican shop. Titto had become obsessed with the gun. He bought a rubber grip for the handle and went as far as getting stars and his name engraved on the side of the gun. The gun became Titto's pride and joy. It never left his side throughout the night or the day. When he could get peace and sleep, he unloaded the gun and slept with it in his hand.

Titto noticed he felt a violent rage raging within himself every time he held the murderous .45 in his hands. Even as a boss now with hired hands to do his bidding, Titto still felt the urge to kill. The .45 compelled him to stay active and make reckless decisions, which endangered the whole operation. It was on one of Titto's reckless, violently influenced missions that he walked right into an FBI undercover sting. One of Titto's men had been pinched making a kilo run from Florida to New Jersey. Titto was tipped off that his worker Ceasar Montez had, without a doubt, turned informant and was trying to run the whole organization. Thanks to his friends at the DEA, Titto was told the man offered the fed's information on his empire and agreed to testify against Titto at the indictment hearing in exchange for his freedom.

The feds kept Ceasar Montez at a safe house in Orlando until the court day, but Titto now had the location of his mark and the time the feds would be transporting him to court. Titto knew he was supposed to pass the hit to others that were willing to eliminate perpetrators, but the .45 willed him, Titto Perez, to execute the rat himself.

What Titto did not know was that he was also under surveillance by the FBI, who was watching, lying in wait to bring him down for a Rico Act violation.

Titto walked to a black van in front of his mansion and got into the rear. One of his most trusted assassins sat in the driver's seat. Titto sat in the back seat, caressing the .45 in his lap as he was chauffeured to an alley in Orlando. The FBI followed closely behind, unaware of what the men in the alley were up to, when Titto and his driver parked. When they got into the alley, the van's driver stepped from the van and walked behind a steel dumpster, which was perched near the back wall of a rundown motel. A black Ford Crown Victoria with tinted windows rolled into the alley and pulled to a stop in front of the motel's back door. The FBI agents took their position at the front of the alley, sensing something was not right and was about to unfold. When the back door of the safe house opened, Titto got out of the van, walked around the van and the undercover Ford sedan to the back door of the safe house, just as Ceasar Montez and an FBI agent stepped out. Titto's gun seemed to appear in his hand almost like a magic act, startling the federal agent. The agent put his hands and arms up to shield his face from the bullets he knew were to come. Titto took aim with the .45, and six bullets spat rapidly through the silencer into the agent's forehead, sending him flying backward and falling dead against the safe house. Next, Titto aimed the pistol at Ceasar Montez's face, pulling the trigger. Four bullets came flying out of the .45's silenced barrel and smashed into Ceasar's face, crushing his nose, mouth, and forehead, making his face look like something out of an old horror movie.

Titto's henchman came from behind the dumpster with an Uzi and opened fire on the other agent as he tried to step out of the car to assist his partner. When Titto's assassin started shooting, his bullets went through the Ford windows, hitting the agent in his torso. The hollow-tip bullets pierced the agent's bulletproof vest, lodging in his lungs.

Titto and his hitman started to walk back to the van, but when they were halfway there, two FBI agents stepped from behind their cover, guns drawn.

"Freeze! FBI! Drop your weapons, Perez!" one of the agents ordered.

Seeing that the agents had the drop on him and that there was no way out the alley without being shot, Titto tried to stop and drop his gun. Titto knew he was done. He knew he was caught. His accomplice looked back and forth between Titto and the agents. Titto started to shake as he tried to control his arm.

"We can take them," the gun said in fact.

"No, no, no, we can't," Titto said, unsure of himself and the gun. The agents watched as Titto spoke to the gun in his hand. "How you going to tell me? You're just a gun! I'm the one that's going to die!" Titto shouted.

Titto lost his battle with the .45 and aimed it at the two agents, who opened fire on both Titto and his accomplice with their service-issued Glock 17 pistols. Titto took one round in the shoulder, which spun him around, and another three slugs in his back. He fell to the gravel in the alley on top of a manhole. His breathing was labored because of the bullets in his lungs. Titto started to suffocate on his own blood. He heard four more gunshots, then he saw his hitman drop to the ground dead next to him. Titto's arm was trapped under his body. He tried to free it and opened the manhole instead. His arm fell into the sewer drain. Titto took his last breath and let the gun fall from his lifeless hand into the Florida sewer system. The sewage current swept the gun away toward a waste dump.

And the saga continues in "The Blower: Part 2" and "The Blower: Part 3" and also "Mary's World" from the author of "Stop Faking For Stripes"—coming soon.

*****Stop Faking For Stripes*****

Growing up on the concrete streets of Los Angeles was a task in itself for most, and for Bobby Lee, it was a hundred times harder. Everything seemed to come harder for Bobby. The drama his best friend from his childhood into his adulthood kept him in had "prison" written all over it. Bobby just wanted to have everything and everybody's respect. He just didn't want to work for it or earn it, even if it killed him or those around him."

*****Sunset*****

Sunset City was almost on the border of California and Mexico. The small city sat right in the center of both countries. It was the perfect city for Umberto and Rodamez Montoya to run their drug operation through. The Montoya cartel had all but cemented themselves as the main suppliers of Sunset, next California.

Kenny Lake wasn't concerned about much but money and drugs. He stayed to his own crew and looked for the big bucks and scores. Nothing else mattered to him but the homes, jewelry, and big-time things that money could buy, so the last thing he wanted to do was get caught up in a drug war with the Montoya Cartel, or anybody else for that matter. Kenny found himself in the middle of two sides that would make him either a hero or a mercenary.

*The Blower: Part 1*****

Titto Perez could not believe what was happening to him whenever he held the gleaming chrome .45 in his hand. It was as though he no longer had control of his arm. He saw the gun come up and open fire on the man he had been sent to kill. He watched the flames explode from out the barrel of the gun, spewing hot automatic lead into his intended target and innocent club goers. Titto stood still in shock for a second, then he remembered he just committed murder in the middle of a nightclub, and walked out with the glowing weapon in his hand.

Printed in the United States
By Bookmasters